The

Vice

President

The

Ten Rules

Written

By

Carolinadeivid

ISBN: 9781916422216
Touchladybirdlucky Studios
A David Gomadza Production.

The Vice President The Ten Rules

DEDICATION

To accountability and the proper use of the world's resources. To a visionary world a world that eradicates misuse but puts more emphasis on the betterment of humanity through the search of new energy sources rather than making weapons. An evil world reversing previous achievements. $$$$ billions spent on making weapons should we not be living up to 200 years. Does the world need a New Driver? The deadliest assassin money can buy. An evil and corrupt world. It's a deadly journey of discovery and danger. A world where evil cults go unchallenged despite the century's gross moral decadence. But one man is sent to cleanse and purge all evil. No one is immune.

DISCLAIMER

This is a work of fiction. Names, characters, businesses, places, events, and incidents are either the products of the author's imagination or used in a fictitious manner. Any resemblance to actual persons, living or dead, or actual events is purely coincidental.

ACKNOWLEDGMENTS

A big thanks to Touchladybirdlucky Studios.

Carolinadeivid

CHAPTER ONE

A cool breeze lifted leaves and all kinds of dirt from the ground into the air. The night was otherwise quiet even though the silence was occasionally interrupted by the sound of dogs barking. A closer look in the dark revealed two shining eyes. A cat dwindled across the field until it came to a road. The cat stopped before crossing the road. Instantly the cat meowed and stopped in the middle of the road. Huge lights blinded it and a huge lorry passed over the cat at a fast speed that the huge tires nearly squashed the cat. Instantly, the cat resumed its journey across the school playground until it came to a residential area. It contortion itself into the yard and across the car park until it reached the closed door. The aerial view of the house showed a huge house, a parked car and the cat running away from the yard. A second level window suddenly opened. A lace curtain dangled outside, inside the bedroom a woman slept peacefully on the bed. Kristi a twenty-six-year-old lady with long spiral hair curls and a curvy body shape with blue eyes were sleeping on the bed. She changed position on the bed and then slept again. Shining eyes caught her attention. An odd-eyed cat, Spooky, three years old, sleeps under the bed before instantly standing up. Two glittering eyes focused on the window. Instant cricket-chirp woke up Kristi. "Get back to sleep Spooky what are you chirping for?" whispered Kristi. Spooky jumped onto the window slab and aggressively scratched the window making cricket-chirps.

"Spooky what is it?" Kristi glanced at the window first then at Spooky.

"You want to go out?" asked Kristi getting up. She entered the kitchen and took cat food and a bowl.

"Here you go, eat, I want to sleep."

Spooky jumped predatory and playfully leaping about on the window slab. He constantly made cricket-chirp sound aggressively. Kristi stealthily got up, scared, she flipped the curtain open and peered outside. She kneeled by the cat and grabbed it. Spooky wriggled making cricket-chirps even louder.

An aerial view showed plain rugged land with what seemed to be blown up vehicles and makeshifts until a huge fence that encompassed what seemed to be a barracks. Soldiers walked around the barracks. An aerial view showed a group of soldiers at a ceremony. A perfect line of army boots came into view. A dozen soldiers or more were on attention all with their right arms raised. They all stood in front of a few uniformed officials. They were making the oath of enlistment. They were all at attention among them Private Brandon, twenty, high and tight hairstyles, green hooded close-set eyes, masculine was at the center of the perfect line. At attention with his hand raised. He cast a serious face eyes fixed at the officials in front of him.

"I private Brandon do solemnly swear...," said Private Brandon.

Instantly an aerial view of all the soldiers at attention before focusing back on Private Brandon.

"... and that I will obey the orders of the President of the United States and the orders of the officers appointed over me," continued Private Brandon.

An eagle circled above the barracks before it suddenly disappeared.

"... So, help me God," swore Private Brandon.

Later the soldiers were gathered around the uniformed officials more relaxed now chatting together, among them was Specialist Hinks.

"Congratulations Private Brandon. It's a great day

for you. The beginning of an interesting career."

Private Brandon smiled and shook hands with the Specialist.

"A great day indeed Specialist."

The soldiers talked over a meal before others arrived.

A car entered the driveway. Kristi opened the door and got out. She walked hastily toward the house. She opened the door and a fresh breeze hit her on her face. She walked into the living room. She stopped and looked at the curtains dancing to the breeze, floating in and out through the window being blown by the wind. She stopped and stared at the open window. She squinted her eyes as if wondering about something.

"Spooky, where are you?" shouted Kristi.

Kristi entered the bedroom. Spooky was licking milk in a bowl. There were two

bowls. Instantly the curtain flipped open and a fresh breeze hit Kristi in the face.

"Did I leave this window open as well?" Questioned Kristi. She glanced and walked to the window. She swiftly flipped open the curtain and scanned outside.

"Spooky did I leave the window open?" asked Kristi looking at Spooky but not

expecting any answers. She pulled the window handle and closed it but stopped and squinted her eyes.

"Why two bowls?"

Kristi scanned the room and spotted milk droplets. She followed the trail of drops to the window slab. She looked outside and cast a haunted face. She then smiled and grabbed the cat before she went into the living room.

Somewhere far away it's night. The frog croaked in a distance. It's dark but the torch of a lit fire lit the otherwise dark night. A well camouflaged, the slithering body came into view and it became clear that it was a soldier. Well camouflaged the soldier stared at the man around the fire. He breathed slowly. Instantly the fire flame reflected in his glittering eyes. Stealthily he pulled his rifle close to his right eye. He squinted his left eye and slowly clipped the trigger.

Somewhere in the city, it's night time. A cat dawdled across the building and disappeared in the dark. Derreck, an ex-soldier, homeless and scruffy slept rough. A siren from far away became more audible. It acted as the film producer's call for action as instantly Derreck got up and sat. A second siren then sends him back into sleep. Another siren woke him up. He instantly sat up.

"Shut up! You son of a bitch!"

A cat jumped up in the dark.

"You! What do you want? Get away from here. I fought for this country and what did I get. The people I fought for are the same people trying to kill me. They are trying to wipe out my memory off. The country I fought for has left me homeless and trampled on all my rights. I swear you make that noise again I will shoot you on the spot you bloody hypocrite son of a...,"

"Shut up you! We are trying to sleep," shouted another man sleeping rough nearby.

"Mind your business. Whose side are you on?" shouted Derreck.

"I fought for this country and what do I have? They are shaking my thighs and my head at the same time all night, so I won't remember anything. Is that fair?" shouted Derreck.

There was a moment of silence.

"I don't care. I want to sleep. Your mistake you trusted these evil crooks. They would rather murder you."

Derreck looked down and touched his head.

"What did you do? I guess all soldiers should be decorated after the war. What is your story? Maybe you did something wrong?" shouted the other homeless person.

"If I am the one who did something wrong, why would they try to wipe out my memory? I think the question is what are they covering up or should I say who are they protecting at my expense?"

"How should I know that? Maybe you were a house burglar how should I know that?"

Derreck looked down for a while.

"I was a real soldier. I made an oath. It makes little sense," shouted Derreck.

"If you are that smart then what are you doing out here. You must have had a big house and a wife somewhere."

Derreck touched the temple of his head and squinted his eyes.

"Wife?" he whispered. He laid down and covered himself in the dark corner.

A car parked outside a huge house and a man got off. He walked swiftly to the house and instantly a woman came out running toward him. A pair of close-set blue eyes with extra mascara cast a flirtatious look before the woman planted a passionate kiss. The man planted back a passionate kiss. The man was Derreck, who laughed and looked down on his side. He kneeled by the cat and picked it up, with clasped hands, the couple strolled away into the house. Derreck woke up and squatted pressing his thighs and groaned in pain. He holds his head, then squinted his eyes and wore an agonized look while crying profusely.

"Evil bastards."

In the other dark corner, a cat meowed and jumped up scared and frightened by the taunting by Derreck. Instantly Derreck wore a dreamy face. He pressed his eyebrows and closed his eyes.

"Damn it. I know that woman."

He pressed his thighs against the leg bones before pressing his side temple. He suffered a severe migraine and cried in agony.

The city was busy even though it was night time. Many people were enjoying the night-life. A couple left the hotel. Ethan, thirty-five years old high taper-fade haircut, average-built with a radiant face, was with his beautiful lady Olivia, twenty-six years old with loose curly side braid and a busty chest. The couple were talking.

"Been a great night, I enjoyed every bit," said Ethan.

Ethan stared at Olivia loathing every bit and ogled her sexy body. Olivia was enjoying every bit of the attention being given to her by Ethan, a rich eligible bachelor.

"Let's spend the night together Ethan. I am all yours," she whispered sexily. Ethan stopped and hugged her by the waist, he kissed her fervently.

"Love to but I can't. I got to go."

Olivia folded her arms and wore a sullen resentful look. She looked down then she stopped walking and looked at Ethan.

"You use me and push me away. Is this what I am to you?" asked Olivia holding Ethan's shoulder.

"I thought what we have is real Ethan," said Olivia.

Ethan smiled and hugged Olivia. He took out a rubber-banded bunch of rolled notes.

He opened the top of Olivia's dress and inserted the bundle between her breasts. He kissed her and smiled.

"You know what? Get a friend and go shopping tomorrow. Come I will drop you off," said Ethan.

He placed his arm around her back and walked her to a parked car. Olivia's face became radiant. She wore a big smile and left a thank you kiss on Ethan's cheek. The couple walked to the car, and the car sped off.

A night bird flew over the plains in the dark, eyes glittering in the dark. It flew over a burning fire. A man sat outside around the fire tossing deadwood into the fire. Around him was a rifle nearby and a kettle. He had bullets around his body. His face said it all. Sullen and bruised with the pain of war, he looked in the burning fire before something startled him. He quickly got up and looked around. He picked up his rifle and walked a few steps ahead. He stopped and stared for a while before walking back and he sat back in his chair. A few miles away a soldier breathed softly holding his breath, he firmly held his rifle. He held in his breath. He aimed the rifle at a man sitting around a fire. Instantly a grasshopper jumped into the air colliding with the barrel of his rifle. That puts him on alert. He froze for a moment and slowly looked at the grasshopper. Briefly, he looked at the grasshopper then back at the man. The man seemed to have heard something as he quickly looked in his direction. The man got up, his rifle in his hand and walked toward the direction the soldier was lying down. The soldier's heartbeat heavily. He slowly investigated the aiming glass of the rifle. He drifted his index finger and held the ring around the trigger. The man seemed to have noticed him, he kept advancing. The soldier's heartbeat increased fast. The soldier clipped the trigger and squinted his eye. The man stopped and stared in his direction. The soldier stared at the man.

"One more step and you are toast," whispered the soldier.

The man seemed to have sensed the danger he stopped and looked in the direction. In the city, a red Ferrari cruised at high speed. Inside was Ethan and Olivia. A Carolinadeivid song Seductive Beauty was playing in the background. Ethan looked at Olivia and smiled. The car screeched its tires around a corner and Ethan pressed the gas pedal harder. He looked at Olivia's legs as her short dress had left her thighs exposed. As soon as Ethan had stuck his eyes on her thighs, she slowly spread her thighs open. She giggled and looked at Ethan.

"Watch it!" she shouted.

Ethan quickly looked in the road ahead of him before he strokes his fingers on Olivia's thigh pushing the short red dress until he can see her white knickers.

"You coming to pick me up tomorrow?" she asked.

Ethan stared on her thighs first. He breathed heavily and gave a quick glance at her before he looked back on the road.

"Honestly I am kind of busy tomorrow but," replied Ethan. Olivia pulled up her dress and revealed her white knickers even further before giggling.

"Yes?" asked Olivia.

Ethan slid his hand between her legs. He instantly cursed and harsh brakes causing the car to skid. The car jerked.

"Oh my God what was that?" shouted Olivia. Ethan looked at Olivia and quickly got out leaving the car door open. He ran back to look. Olivia looked back through the rear window screen and saw Ethan kneeling by what seemed to be a man or animal in the road. She quickly cast a fear-creased face. She was anxious. Ethan quickly jumped back into the car and drove off.

"What was that?" asked Olivia.

Ethan cast a haunted face and glanced at Olivia and drove off silently. Olivia got attracted to the blood spot on Ethan's jeans. She looked at his face, but he did not look back he kept staring at the road ahead of him.

At night the light rays of the lamp post outside reflected in the bedroom. Lying on the bed Kristi smiled, her eyes drifted beneath closed eyelids. Instantly she snapped open her eyelids and pulled down her knickers. She slid her hand down before sobbing herself to sleep. Spooky jumped onto the bed and slept next to her. Kristi felt a cool breeze on her face. She slowly opened her eyes.

"Spooky get down. I want to sleep," she whispered.

She stretched her hand looking for the cat with her eyes closed. She snapped opened her eyes. Instantly a cool breeze blew on her.

"Spooky!"

She raised her head and peered outside the window briefly before the cat meowed under the bed. A strange feeling paralyzed her. She got up and closed the window and slept.

Miles away in the nearby suburb a house nearby has a light lit on in one bedroom. Inside the bedroom Specialist Hinks, twenty-three years old, burr cut, masculine slept fidgeting on the bed. He was having a nightmare. He turned his head fast left then right. His eyes were moving under his closed eyelids. He was sweating, his face showing an agonized and tormented face.

"No, No. No!"

Instantly he snapped-opened his eyelids and pressed hard his thigh muscles and screamed in agony. He pressed his side temple as if having a migraine. He lay on top of the bed and searched the table with a stretched hand. He retrieved his rosary and put it on before he slept again. Somewhere far away in the forests of a foreign country. The soldier aimed his rifle lying down on his stomach. His index finger tightly gripped on the trigger. The man miles away around a fire instantly stopped and removed the rifle from his shoulder. Instantly a bullet blasted open his left chest blowing him backward. The soldier cocked up the rifle again before a loud scream sliced the otherwise silent night. The soldier quickly slumped down looking up in the sky. A scream by a boy caused his heartbeat to beat quick. The aerial view showed a young boy kneeling by the man and the fire burning beside them.

In the house in the nearby suburb Specialist, Hinks squinted his eyes in front of the bathroom mirror. He doused his face with water. He looked at himself in the mirror. He stood there for a while. A lot of thoughts were running in his head. Why all these nightmares? Since returning from the tour of duty the nightmares had become more pronounced worst more when he doesn't have the rosary. He breathed heavily and walked back into the bedroom. He lay on the bed facing up. He slept on top of the bed before he searched the table with a stretched hand. He retrieved his rosary and wore it. A few days later Specialist Hinks was training with Corporal Aiden, twenty-five, burr cut, masculine and with deep-set eyes. The Corporal lunged and kneed Specialist Hinks in the rib cage. He kicked him on the shoulder that caused him to stagger backward. He then ferociously lunged forward and backfired a series of kicks using both legs. Corporal Aiden blocked all attacks before he attacked himself. He threw the front jab, the cross, the hook, and the huddle so fast leaving the Specialist in agony. The Specialist staggered backward but attacked, throwing a series of kicks leaving the Corporal nursing his ribs.

"Since coming back, I haven't been myself. I have horrible nightmares," said

Specialist Hinks. The Corporal stopped and laughed

rubbing off sweat from his face.

"Is that an excuse or you want to end the game whilst you are still winning?" the Corporal taunts the Specialist who cast a haunted look. He breathed heavily.

"Seriously. I feel like there are voices in my head. I nearly lost my leg the other night,"

replied the Specialist.

The Corporal walked close to the Specialist and grabbed his shoulder.
"This job is not for the weak. Find a way of controlling these nightmares," advised the Corporal.

The two men walked toward the bench.

"You must go back out there, with time all this will go away," said the Corporal. The Specialist cast a quizzed face. He breathed heavily and wiped the sweat from his face.

"You know what? Once I wear the rosary all this stop isn't that funny?" said the Specialist.

The Corporal took a towel and doused off the sweat from his face. He smiled and looked at the Specialist.

"What you need is a medal. Remember this is not just a medal. It protects me. It could have been even harder without it. I never take mine off," explained the Corporal. He flipped up his t-shirt to reveal a medal of honor underneath. He touched it and smiled.

"One day you might say differently Specialist," added the Corporal.

"Until next time," remarked the Specialist.

A well-built man, Mason, thirty-seven years old with a burr cut hairstyle stopped and scanned the area. He pulled the dog belt. A huge tailless dog followed him sniffing everywhere. The huge gates slowly opened, and a twenty-eight years old woman walked into the building. Inside a huge dog stood up as the door opened. A beautiful average-built lady, Layla walked in wearing reading glasses and a white overall. She kneeled by the dog and rubbed the dog.

"Hey boy," she said looking at Evan, in his forties, wearing reading glasses. He was medium built and was reading a report.

"Failure!"

"Are you sure?" asked Layla surprised.

"What else did you expect? You are trying to play God. Just not good enough,"

remarked Evan. Layla looked unimpressed and walked toward Evan.

"In theory, it works," replied Layla.

"Please for Christ's sake. The device destroys otherwise good genes," exclaimed Evan highly disapproving.

"This is the future Evan, after all, it is still the early stages, but I believe the future is bright," explained Layla.

Evan cast a disapproving face. Layla smiled and cast a radiant face.

"Even though sperm production is increased, the sperm is abnormal, with missing or altered genes talking about genetic disorders," quipped Evan. He shook his head in disapproval and twisted his lips.

"All the babies to be born to these subjects will have genetic defects. Trust me this will never work unless you want to create more jobs," said Evan.

Layla stopped and looked at Evan. She then walked closer to Evan and leaned forward.

"Give it a chance the medical device will work," requested Layla.

"This is not just playing God, but you are being the ruthless devil himself," Evan sighed heavily.

"If mankind was scared as you, surely, we could not have achieved all this," remarked Layla.

"You can't tell me that when it takes days to manufacture healthy sperm naturally, this device will produce good quality sperm in hours. That is just impossible," explained Evan.

"Why not?" asked Layla removing her reading glasses.

Evan looked disappointed and upset.

"Look at the results of the DNA genetic structure. A lot of strands are damaged or missing some parts. This is clear evidence that this medical device is not just a failure but will cause unforeseen genetic disorders among all newborn babies."

Layla wriggled her mouth and wore back her reading glasses.

"Evan, it's not that bad. Just early stages. We need more research and tests before we can conclude," pleaded Layla.

"Speaking of high disability rates. Even if the children survive the suicides, rates will be higher among them. Gender-related problems will also be common if not persistent among the offspring. You know all this and if you know all this then why you persist in defending something that will rack lives like that?"

Evan squinted his eyes twisting his lower lip.

"You are deliberately trying to cause all this? Political thing ha? Increased health budget and more jobs? How do you sleep at night?" asked Evan upset.

CHAPTER TWO

In the forests of a foreign country, the loud cries of a boy deafened the noises made by the night creatures. The fire near him rages as it burns violently with the cool breeze blowing the fire flames. The boy was kneeling by the man who was lying on the ground. A rifle was next to him. The boy had just left the nearby building after hearing a gunshot sound only to find the man almost dead in a pool of blood. The young boy horrified looked at his hands shocked by the amount of blood and confused he screamed before he took the rifle and cocked it and fired bullets in the surrounding bushes. He kneeled by the dead man and removed the belt of bullets. He wiped tears whilst loading the rifle. A few meters away the soldier got up and walked away stealthily. The cries of a young boy sliced the otherwise silent night this startled the soldier who stealthily walked away ducking like an early man. Staggering away. He still could hear the boys' cries and the cricket chirping in the surrounding bushes. A bullet tore through his side stomach that he fell to the ground. His rifle fell feet away. He crawled toward the rifle. He could hear the cries of the boy becoming increasingly audible. He panicked and grabbed his rifle. He groaned in agony and looked at his hand covered in blood. A gunshot sound sends him ducking. He staggered away and hid behind a tree and closed his eyes. He gathered his energy and aimed the rifle. Moments later the soldier could hear the frogs croak before a crackling radio sound from Eagle, a carpet bomber startled him. "Receiving loud and clear," said the soldier.

"Approaching clear the area. Have to blanket-sweep the area," said the operator from the bomber.

"Negative! Abort there are civilians. I repeat civilians. Abort!" shouted the soldier.

In the city it's sunny and the roads are jammed with traffic. Specialist Hinks was with Corporal Aiden. The background music was Angels on Earth by Carolinadeivid.

Background song.

Will you protect me? Will you save me?

I should protect you from above. Yet I am an angel on earth.

The Corporal tapped his fingers on the steering wheel. He looked outside and ahead before looking at the Specialist.

"How are the nightmares?" asked the Corporal.

"Some days it's better but my legs are giving me much pain. Been to the doc everything is OK," remarked the Specialist.

"It's a war Specialist and better than being dead," he looked in the road ahead.

"I am afraid not. It's not the war or combat. My problems started when I came back," explained the Specialist.

Silence sliced through and only the background song can be heard.

"You must go back there. Until you have a medal of honor, that's when everything will stop. Life will be easy," said the Corporal.

The Specialist glanced outside before a man appeared in front of the car nearly getting knocked down by the SUV.

"Watch it fool!" shouted the Specialist.

The Specialist cursed at the homeless scruffy man.

The Corporal opened the glove compartment and drove a few feet ahead and gave money to the man. The Specialist's lips curled contemptuously.

"Lazy bastard!" shouted the Specialist.

The Corporal laughed and pointed in the rear-view mirror. The Specialist removed his sunglasses and glanced for a while. Instantly the man saluted at attention and cast a serious face. Shocked and surprised the Specialist looked at the Corporal.

"Is he one of us?" asked the Specialist.

"They told him they were helping him forget, to stop the nightmares," said the Corporal a little upset.

"So?" asked the Specialist.

"They mashed up his brain and branded him an Oxygen-thief," said the Corporal.

The Specialist cast an agonized look.

"These lying evil bastards. I think it's them deliberately causing these nightmares. They only started after I felt my thighs vibrating followed by a migraine," exclaimed the Specialist.

The Corporal shrugged, one hand on the steering

wheel. He looked at the Specialist and raised his eyebrows as if saying even myself I can't believe it.

"That's what they call therapy?"

"Therapy my ass? It's them trying to damage my brain. That thing won't stop rotating. They said it was to protect us." The Specialist cursed and glanced outside.

"Is this protection? Just imagine I nearly sacrificed my life only to be brain damaged by them. Is this not betrayal Corporal?"

"For him, it's too late. He is just waiting to be auctioned," Specialist Hinks cast a forced smile and sniffled.

"You make me laugh. Why joke with something like this?" The Corporal cast a serious haunted look.

"You are joking right?"

"Only a medal can protect you," said the Corporal.

The Specialist's facial expressions changed to incredulity.

"That's bullshit. The government must protect these men. We took an oath to serve this country to die for this country yet after we return, we have nothing ending up living on the streets," said the Specialist.

"He did not get a medal?"

"Not for everyone," said the Corporal.

The Corporal looked ahead and drove the car.

"The medal safeguards you. Gives you protection. Easy access to the bank mortgage, retraining and a steady income," added the Corporal.

"But they say the medals have no monetary value and can't be sold how can these medals safeguard you?" asked the Specialist.

"You are asking me that? Have your nightmares stopped?" asked the Corporal.

Kristi was sleeping peacefully on the bed. Suddenly she felt a cold breeze and

shivered. She pulled extra bed linen. She felt the cat jumped on the bed. Spooky

meowed in her face. She opened her eyes.

"What is it?"

Spooky jumped off the bed and onto the window

slab and scratched the window playfully making cricket-chirps. Predatory the cat moved from one end to the other as if following a flying butterfly or insect outside the window. The cat jumped back onto the bed and meowed looking at the window. Scared but highly curious Kristi looked on.

"No. It's freezing. We can't open the window."

The cat jumped back onto the window slab. Kristi looked on before dozing off. She felt the cat jumping and climbing on her but instantly she felt sudden shivering. She felt the cat on top of her. She opened her eyes and saw the cat on the floor drinking milk.

"Then who is on top of me?" Kirsti asked herself thinking out loud. She raised her head, and that's when all her hairs rose. Instantly something jumped down and sprinted outside through the open window. Kirsti quickly flipped the curtain open and scanned outside and closed the window. She realized she had closed the window before. A scream sliced the otherwise silent night waking up all the neighbors. A large crowd had gathered in the conference room. The Atmosphere said it all, something big was on the cards. Mr. Chunks in his fifties with gray hair of slim build with dark circles-under-eyes was in the room together with the journalist and the photographers who all filled the room. Mr. Chunks re-positioned his tie after getting up and looked at everyone.

"Today is a great stride for mankind. Gone are the days when we will leave things to chance," he paused and looked at the crowd.

"Ladies and gentlemen this small device (raised a doubled-capsule sized instrument) will revolutionize humanity as we know it."

He glanced at the crowd and his chin was raised high oozing with confidence.

"Diseases, aging, wrinkles, genetic disorders, you name it are all going to be the things of the past," he paused and looked at everyone. He cast a radiant look but this time with little conviction and belief, he continued.

"Having said that this doesn't come cheap. But the good news is that we have planned it all with the banks and all loan providers. We have made arrangements that will make it easy for every one of you to gain this device. Everyone looked attentively before an outburst broke out. The reporters talked to themselves, among them is Dick, a thirty-four-year-old reporter with short curled-hair, long-faced and strong-jawed. He looked troubled for a minute before he raised his hand and asked a question.

"Mr. Chunks are you trying to play God or the devil himself?"

Everyone looked at each other without a word.

"We are trying to safeguard our health and our way of life if that means playing God so be it," remarked Mr. Chunks.

A huge buzz filled the conference room. Mr. Dick stared at everyone and then glanced at Mr. Chunks.

"What are the side effects? I understand you are just going ahead despite the failures observed in the trials?"

Mr. Chunks stepped in front closer to Mr. Dick. He stopped and looked at everyone first. He then cast his eyes at Mr. Dick.

"Let me say this. No system is perfect. We weighed the benefits over the cost and I can say we believe this will bring tremendous benefits," said Mr. Chunks not convincing anyone. His voice patterns showed stress patterns. Mr. Dick looked disappointed.

He breathed heavily.

"Do you think man-made genetic disorders are

even tolerated no matter what the benefits are? Isn't that playing stupid and recklessly with the people's lives?" asked Mr. Dick. Mr. Chunk remained silent for a while. He wiped the sweat droplets from his face.

"Let me say that we are determined to deliver the goods and the best results. We will do our best," replied Mr. Chunks.

Mr. Dick shook his head in disbelief and anger. As soon as he spoke his anger was revealed by his voice patterns.

"Tell me what exactly are you trying to do? Best to do what? Replace natural processes with these man-made devices. Do you know this device is the one causing all these genetic disorders? Considering that then I ask you. What are your real intentions?"

A huge buzz filled the whole conference room. People talked to themselves ignoring calls by Mr. Chunks to be silent. Mr. Chunks shaken stood there in front of the people speechless. He changed position in front of the crowd. He could read the anger on people's faces. He knew he had to play his cards right. He gathered his nerves and walked towards Mr. Dick.

"What do you mean Mr. Dick?" he asked.

Mr. Dick wore an aggressive look. His face creased up with anger. He knew deep down that Mr. Chunks knew exactly what he was talking about. He knew the world had been deceived and had been hand given cookies by Mr. Chunks to even bother raising the fundamental questions. Casting an annoyed upset look, he quizzed Mr. Chunks.

"Is this your idea of creating more jobs in your government? Honestly, that's the only reason that makes sense unless if you can convince me otherwise."

The crowd went crazy as there was a huge buzz.

"Yes, tell us Mr. Chunks, what is your real motive? Ha?"

Mr. Chunks stopped still for a minute or two. He looked upset this time.

"Watch it! Watch your mouth, okay," shouted Mr. Chunks.

"Ladies and gentlemen, I have just found out they implanted this device when my baby girl was born and deliberately rotated it nonstop. Ladies and gentlemen this device is the one that caused horrific injuries to her body until the day she died."

Silence filled the conference room.

"Ladies and gentlemen, I want to clarify that Mr. Dick's daughter was born with a genetic disorder. After seeking our help, we used the device to help her," justified Mr. Chunks.

A short outburst filled the conference room before Mr. Dick broke the silence. He looked downbeat than before. His eyes to those near him were glittering with tears.

He looked down and took out a small picture from his wallet. He looked at it and looked at the crowd.

"Ladies and gentlemen, myself and my wife we are the first victims of Mr. Chunks," he looked at everyone. A huge buzz filled the conference room as the crowd went berserk.

"Yes, without our given consent they raped us in the name of research. Yes, Mr.

Chunks' doctors abused their position. This is worse because these people are in a position of trust, therefore, more trust and honesty are expected of them. In this light I will honestly say we were grossly abused in broad daylight by Mr. Chunks and his doctors," he paused and breathed heavily. Everyone looked and focused.

"They shook us using this propelled device and electronically using an inserted electrode-needle stimulated our nerves to increase sperm and egg production using this device. So, in light of this, I ask you if it is not reasonable to say the resultant baby had genetic disorders?"

A huge outburst filled the room. Mr. Chunks looked at the crowd and saw most people nodding their heads in agreement. His heartbeat shot sky-high. He looked down for a while. He looked at Mr. Dick and sighed.

"We are not God? I am not God. The medical device was used to correct the problems caused by a genetic disorder and we tried to help," explained Mr. Chunks.

The crowd waited patiently to hear what Mr. Dick would say.

"Ladies and gentlemen, if the device can imitate the body's good system and functions like fighting disease what stops the same device from imitating the bad conditions or causing the bad conditions? Don't be fooled by Mr. Chunks and his team. They are trying to make the whole thing sound like what came out first in the egg-and-hen situation. This is not the case. This is a clear-cut case. The baby had genetic disorders because they played God and tampered with the parent's reproductive system."

The crowd went berserk. A huge buzz filled the room. Mr. Dick was so far winning the argument. The crowd saw why Mr. Dick was adamant that Mr. Chunks was all along responsible for all the problems from day one even though he tried to pretend to help.

This was a clear causal-effect relationship.

"We can only see smoke when there is a fire. These two cannot be separated from each other because they depend on each other. Ladies and gentlemen, Mr. Chunks and his government are not just playing God but the devil himself. Too much pain and suffering so they can increase jobs. They say: why not cause more diseases, have more people with genetic disorders then provide people with jobs? Who on earth would do such a thing? Who on earth would tolerate something like this?"

Everyone looked at Mr. Chunks who was finding it hard to breathe. He forced himself to talk, shaking with anger.

"Mr. Dick be careful what you say!" shouted Mr. Chunks.

Mr. Dick looked upset himself. He creased his face with rage and looked at

Mr. Chunks.

"Or what Mr. Chunks? Kill my daughter for the second time or kill me? Or get me struck by the lightning again?" asked Mr. Dick.

Mr. Dick removed his cap and revealed a balding head. Some reporters laughed as they saw Mr. Dick's balding head. Mr. Chunks briefly laughed and instantly looked down forcing himself hard not to laugh.

"Please! Mr. Dick. First, I apologize for your loss but it's just absurd that you suggest that I am responsible for the lightning that struck you causing you baldness, this is just preposterous," quipped Mr. Chunks.

Mr. Dick walked in front of everyone and bent down and asked everyone to look at his head. Everyone shouted in disbelief. Mr. Dick's face instantly slumped. Everyone looked at Mr. Chunks. If eyes could stab and kill someone, I think this day, most would have sliced him to death in seconds. Mr. Dick wiped tears down his cheek.

"You can see for yourself this is another of their games. Look closely at the balding pattern. What do you see?" asked Mr. Dick before instantly interrupted by Mr. Chunks.

"Ladies and gentlemen please ignore that I am sure that has nothing to do with us.

Mr. Dick is grieving and want to point fingers," shouted Mr. Chunks.

" A minute ago, Mr. Chunks was sure this was a natural thing and now," said Mr. Dick before being interrupted by another reporter.

A woman reporter got up her name was Yunis, thirty-nine-years-old, a brunette with smooth and straight hair.

"Mr. Dick your story is hard to believe. If Mr. Chunks' doctors raped, you as you call it why didn't you go to the police or report them? Grief for your loss can make you easily point fingers," said Yunis. Mr. Dick wiped a tear down his cheek.

"Mrs.?" asked Mr. Dick.

"Yunis, Mr. Dick," replied Yunis.

"Look closely what does that resemble? Is this how people bald? They fried me one night only to wake up like this. Imagine what they can do? The time you will believe me it will be too late," said Mr. Dick.

"What does that resemble? I can't see anything

apart from a lovely balding head," said Yunis laughing. She looked at the crowd hoping they will all join her in mocking Mr. Dick, but the people had understood Mr. Dick's argument. They had seen evil in broad daylight.

"Mrs. Yunis. Don't be a smart-ass. Have you seen the marks left by an electronic-killing chair I mean that metal plate they put on the head of the person they are electrocuting to death?"

The silence broke out and Yunis realized that she had been very slow to understand. Mr. Chunks was bad to the bone than eyes could see. After all, Mr. Dick had a compelling case against what he called evil. Mr. Dick bent his head and showed even Mr. Chunks who remained silent for a while.

"Yes, you said the balding was natural what about now?" asked Mr. Dick.

Yunis pulled her lips in shock when she realized what was happening.

"Mr. Chunks are you threatening me with death if I keep protesting. They are frying me in broad daylight saying that they have the backing of even the leader of this country. Okay, I ask another question Mrs. Yunis, have you been mouse-trapped-blind before as they call it?" asked Mr. Dick. Yunis did not reply but just sat down. "They are using this device to terrorize the people. They are blinding people at will, mouse-trapping them as they call it and blackmailing us, so we can't complain. They used the device to make my wife a horny freak making her horny twenty-four-hours a day to destroy her credibility," remarked Mr. Dick.

A huge buzz instantly filled the room.

"They are using this device to reverse everything," he paused and glanced down and wiped another tear.

"You all know you can take out petrol from a car tank by siphoning, yes?" asked Mr. Dick.

The crowd agreed.

"That's how they used this device on my daughter, siphoning fluids using air pressure and circulating this in her body until the day she died. Who on earth would do that apart from this evil, Mr. Chunks?" said Mr. Dick trembling with rage.

Everyone looked at Mr. Chunks, but he remained silent.

"It does not stop there; this device is being used also to wipe out memory. The device vibrates like a cell phone continuously shaking one's brain for hours until its jelly. Can you not say this is inhumane beyond any human circles? Who on earth would do something like this?

It's a beautiful sunny day. The local restaurant is packed with people enjoying the day.

Specialist Hinks is sitting on the table with Corporal Aiden. Among them also is Private Barnes twenty-one of age with a burr cut hairstyle. He has deep-set eyes. Also, with them is Private Flipper twenty years old with a crew cut hairstyle.

"What I don't understand is why these medals of honor protect us? Do I have to wear this everywhere?" asked the Specialist.

"I haven't got one yet, is that why these nightmares won't go away?" Private Barnes cast an inquisitive look.

"Once I got my medal everything was back to normal. Life was better for me. I had billionaires offering to buy the medal," said the Corporal.

"What's the catch? These medals are valueless why would someone pay a lot of money? Something just does not seem right," said the Specialist. He cast a skeptical and doubtful look. The other men looked at Private flipper who remained silent for a while when everyone expected him to contribute to the conversation.

"Fortunately for me, I don't have nightmares," said Private Flipper calmly. The other soldiers looked at each other in shock.

"Private Flipper what makes you so special?" asked the Corporal.

Private Flipper cheekily smiled and looked at the other soldiers.

"How am I supposed to know that?" he asked as all the three men stared at each other.

"What do we have in common the three of us?" asked the Specialist.

CHAPTER THREE

Somewhere in the city, a large crowd had gathered outside a government building with placards and posters. People were fighting with the security service and among them was Lily a thirty-four-year-old with short fluffy hair and big bulging hazel eyes. "The government is causing untold genetic disorders just to create jobs and justify the huge budget; this is inhumane and absurd. We want them to be held accountable for the suffering of every woman and child." The crowd applauded hysterically.

"It's time we hold them to account. They can't do like King Herod, who used midwives and illegally implanted medical devices and tagged innocent young infants then abused them in later years!" shouted Lily.

Security was tight outside a huge government building. There were a lot of cars outside and a man appeared from one of the building corners. He stopped and whispered something in his left shoulder before a cracking-noise startled a passerby who briefly stopped before continuing to the gate. The passerby a woman probably in her late thirties entered the huge fence. After being cleared she entered the huge building. Inside was well decorated, and this building housed a very important person, the President. A tall man around fifty-two-years old with a low taper-fade cut hairstyle, and a masculine defined body is in the office. His look emitted confidence and high esteem. The way he walked defined authority. He stood in his office and walked to the window and glanced outside. A knock at the door startled him briefly.

The Vice President a beautiful elegant woman with more self-esteem than anyone you have ever met entered the office. A woman in her early forties with short curly-hair and green glittering eyes. The two sighed briefly.

"I don't know how we let it go this far?" said the President.

"How were we supposed to know?" replied Mrs. Vice President.

"A lot on the table right now. The likelihood of a war, uprising at home and dwindling coffers," added the President.

Silence broke out for a while.

"We need to clean this mess first," replied the Vice President.

The sound of stilettos or high heels can be heard from a distance and the noise gradually becomes audible. Rex peeked outside of his office to see who it was. He saw a beautiful woman with a short dress stopping and kneeling to pick a small paper she had just dropped. The woman continued walking toward him before he withdraws his head and disappeared. As the woman was passing his office, she knocked on the door but continued walking. A few steps away from the door a voice shouted in the corridor. She swerved and twisted her body instantly facing the way she came.

"What is it?" shouted Rex.

"Conference time let's go. I don't want to be late," replied Stacy.

"Okay wait for me, will you?"

The woman stopped for a while but as soon as Rex's head disappeared from his door the woman walked fast and disappeared around the corner. She entered the conference room. The place was filled with journalists and reporters. The President was about to answer questions after addressing the nation. Enoch thirty-eight years old a handsome man with a taper-fade haircut is among the reporters. After everyone had seated the President took center stage.

"We have a moral obligation to go to war and protect the rights of those affected no matter how harsh it may sound. We pledged to defend the powerless and nothing will change that," quipped the President.

"Mr. President, what is your real motive? Most people believe you are going to war to steal the resources of other countries," asked Enoch.

There was a huge buzz as the people laughed. The President smiled and looked at everyone.

"If that means providing peace and the upholding of human rights, so be it," replied the President.

A huge noise echoed in the room that the President stopped addressing the reporters and journalists. Stacy looked outside from afar and saw a crowd gathered outside holding posters and banners. Brian the human rights campaigner a thirty-four years old man was addressing the crowd.

"It's just coming to light it seems this medical device has altered the genetic makeup of mankind, we don't know the numbers yet, but it doesn't look good," he glanced down at the crowd.

"It's that bad that now it's rare to find 'pure people' with their unaltered natural genetic make-up still intact. This device not only damaged good genes but caused severe mutations of otherwise normal genes," explained Brian. The crowd shouted and chanting.

"We want an end to all this. We want these evil monsters to be held accountable," shouted the crowd.

"It does not stop there. Using these medical devices, they have created viruses. Yes, man-made lethal viruses which they are loading our women and kids and deciding how and when they die through this device," argued Brian.

Kaydence looked into the rear-view mirror and smiled. He looked outside the car through the window and saw a gorgeous tall lady walking on the pavement. He looked at her and smiled. She looked at him before the driver behind abruptly blasted the car horn.

"Jesus did you have to do that?" said Kaydence waiting for the car in front to drive off.

Quickly he turned on the radio and looked in the

rear-view mirror.

Voice on the radio caught his attention.

'Since introducing these medical devices normal people have become rare. The world waged war after war killing each other. Diseases had ravaged the people. It was like back in the old days with the population riddled with man-made viruses. The medical devices malfunctioned, and people would explode like bombs, so the people thought but in fact, this was intentional. Humankind was headed for extinction as the device after implantation became part of the nervous system meaning they could not be removed.'

"Jesus who would do such a thing?" shouted Kaydence to himself.

A woman strolled in the corridor before stopping outside one of the offices. A quick knock on the door and she entered the office. Her name was Kaylee a thirty-one-year-old with short hair and lovely close-set eyes. She pushed the heavy door and looked inside first before walking toward the desk. Inside are other people among them the Professor, an old man in his late fifties with gray hair. Also, there are security officers, the President himself and the Vice President too.

"Mr. President we believe we have found an

antidote. This person has shown near to human genetic makeup. Somehow the device is not causing any mutations," explained Kaylee with confidence and happy to deliver hope in such circumstances.

The president sighed a little skeptical.

"Do you know why?" asked the President.

"No, we have no clue why that is so. All tests were normal. We don't know if this has to do with the fact that he is a billionaire," explained the Professor.

"A billionaire? So, money can stop these mutations?" asked the Vice President.

She glanced at the President with the corner of her eyes and sighed pondering about all this.

"Have you checked other billionaires?" asked the President.

"We checked but no one similar to him," replied the Professor.

"Then find out more about him before jumping into conclusion," said the President walking out of the office.

A few days later the Vice President and the President are talking in the Presidential office. The atmosphere was relaxed a little.

"Mr. President a ray of hope for mankind would you say?" asked the Vice President.

"There have been benefits too. Do you know that? People nowadays live longer just these genetic mutations. If we do nothing, we will lose support," explained the President.

"Hospitals full of people with these genetic disorders," said the Vice President

shrugging her shoulders. The President looked down and breathed heavily.

"It was a good idea at first driving our campaign, providing jobs and justifying the huge budget and driving the economy. It was a win-win for everyone. I don't know what happened," said the President sounding stressed and hopeless.

"What if that happened to your son or daughter will you let them suffer like that just so we remain in power?" asked the Vice President walking toward the window.

She looked outside expecting an answer from the President. She turned around and looked at the

President. The President slumped into his seat and he could only stare at the Vice President. An SUV screeched its tires around a corner before it disappeared in the city center.

Later the SUV appeared in one street in the city before coming to a halt outside a flat in the city center. Brayden age forty-one-year-old masculine and armed was in the SUV among him was Tyler aged thirty-five with a fresh crew cut hairstyle. He was of average-built and highly armed too. In the back seat was Adrian aged twenty-nine with an undercut hairstyle masculine and armed too. As soon as the SUV came to a stop, the men got off and slammed the doors closed. They stood outside one flat. A light was on in one bedroom. The men stood outside looking. Inside the flat was Olivia is with Tristan aged twenty-six with a straight low fade haircut. The couple were watching the television when a knock startled them. They threw each other a quick glance.

"Are you expecting someone," quizzed Tristan sacred and worried.

Olivia shook her head and walked to the door.

"Mrs. Olivia can we talk?" asked Brayden as Olivia slightly opened the door. The men flashed their badges.

Olivia hesitated but Tristan pulled the door open.

"Who is this?" asked Brayden pointing at Tristan but Dominic interrupted before Olivia had the chance to reply.

"You can let us in, or you can come with us," he explained.

Olivia hesitated.

"It's regarding what?" she asked.

"Ethan," replied Adrian with a strong hoarse voice.

Olivia removed the chain-lock and slowly opened the door.

The men walked inside.

Tristan looked worried and sounded jealous. He looked at Olivia.

"Who? Ethan the Ethan? Are you still seeing that cunt?" asked Tristan.

"Go I will call you Tristan OK?" said Olivia pushing Tristan toward the door. The men looked at each other.

"On second thought, I think he should stay if he

feels this way about Ethan," maybe he can help us. A breeze blew the grass and trees in the cemetery. The place was deserted apart from the presence of a woman kneeling near a grave. It's sunny though even with this warm breeze. A bird chirped and flew from the tree landing at the grave's pillar. The woman in black removed her sunglasses. It's Kristi. She looked haunted and sad.

"Darling is that you? I don't know what to think. A lot is happening at home which I can't explain," she said pruning the grave. She sounded upset and stressed up as revealed by her voice patterns.

In the evening Rex a man in his thirties with a straight low fade taper hairstyle and a well masculine built body was in the house. Titus thirty-five years old his best friend with a burr haircut also masculine was with him. The two were seated in the lounge.

Kristi entered with cold drinks. She sat down and sighed.

"So, this is about Derreck, right?" asked Titus.

"I don't know what to say without sounding...," said Kristi without finishing her

sentence.

"So, what are you saying?" asked Rex.

Kristi cast a haunted look.

"I think Derreck is alive or somehow, he is trying to communicate with me. Strange things have been happening lately.

Titus sat up straight and looked Kristi straight into her eyes.

"What strange things?" he asked instantly.

Kristi paused for a while.

"I felt someone on the bed the other day," said Kristi not that convincing.

Instantly Spooky meowed and jumped onto the sofa.

Rex smiled and grabbed the cat.

"There is your answer. Speaking of the devil," replied Rex.

Every smiled. Kristi hugged and kissed the cat.

"I don't think he died like they said. A few days ago, a bird flew and landed on the grave's pillar not bothered by my presence at all. I found that strange," explained Kristi.

"What are you suggesting?" asked Rex.

The following days the group talked together on the phone. Then one night two cars parked outside Kristi's house. Rex jumped into Titus' SUV as well as Kristi. Later the SUV entered the graveyard sending a cloud of dust into the air. The SUV then parked near a grave. After a while, Kristi is in the SUV seated in the back seat looking at the two men, Rex, and Titus who were digging up the grave. The SUV's lights were flashing at the two men.

Kristi looked around the graveyard. A shadow caught her attention. She felt sacred for a split-second but the thought of it being Derreck calmed her down. She looked at the two men. In her mind, a lot of questions were going through. She was busy thinking about this ordeal when she noticed the two men stopped and stared at each other. The two men glanced at each other and looked at the SUV. Kristi got the message and got out. She got out and stood in front of the SUV. The only thing they could hear were night crickets chirping from a distance.

"Open it," whispered Kristi but loud enough for the two to have heard.

Hesitantly the men open the coffin. Kristi leaned

forward but couldn't see. She looked at the two men. She opened her eyes. The men just looked at each other and then at her without a word.

"You are killing me. Tell me, is he there?"

The two men threw each other a quick glance.

Somewhere far away a car entered a huge steel gate. The man entered the building. He walked the long corridors passing several rooms. He greeted a man who entered one of the rooms. Inside the room is the Professor he looked at him and soon after he left the room, into the lift and straight into the lab. Kaylee entered the lab and greeted the Professor. She looked surprised to find the President and the Vice President in there already.

"So, what are you saying?" asked the President.

"Up to now we don't know the main reason, but the interesting thing is that he is possessed," said the Professor.

The President cast a quizzical look.

"Are you telling me that the two most renowned scientists of our time would believe that?" asked the President.

"The only explanation is that somehow he has

other people or something within him that is changing the behavior of the medical device. It is imitating whatever is within him," replied Kaylee.

The President sensed Kaylee's crackling voice patterns straight away he became

skeptical.

"If that's just imitating, then it could just be a short-term thing," said the President.

"The mutations are clearing. Somehow it is reversing the bad genes," replied the Professor.

The President walked to the window and glanced outside.

"All these years we thought we were heading for extinction, at last, there is something to smile about," said the President smiling.

"Have we tried removing this device?" asked the Vice President.

"Yes, but with severe results, from the day it's implanted it seemed it merged with the nervous system and permanently became the person's nervous system," replied the Professor.

"We need to act fast. Some have exploded like

bombs," explained the Professor.

"Exploding?" asked the President.

A knock on the door startled everyone.

"Yes. What do you have for us?" asked the President.

"He had a hit and run," replied Brayden.

"How is that related to this?" asked the Vice President.

"He killed a homeless man," replied Adrian.

"Did you check him Professor?" asked the Vice President.

The President looked worried.

"What do we know about this homeless man?" asked the President.

A cat walked outside one of the houses in one of the suburbs. It stopped outside and looked back before walking away. The lights in the house were on. Inside the lounge room was Rex, Titus, and Kristi.

"What do you suggest?" asked Rex.

"Where do we start?" added Titus.

"I think there is a lot we don't know. Honestly whoever is behind this has a plan for us too," suggested Rex.

"Rex is right. I think it will be safe for you to leave this to us," remarked Titus.

Kristi sniffled.

"What are you saying? He was my fiancé," asked Kristi.

Rex breathed heavily and leaned forward toward Kristi.

"Listen whoever is behind this has more power it will be safe for you to pretend that everything is okay. Leave this to me and Titus. OK?" requested Rex.

Many people were sitting down on chairs in a perfect line. There was a huge tent outside with a PA system. A siren became audible and the sound gradually increased.

A motorcade parked behind the tent and the President and his bodyguards got out and walked toward the tent. Many people were seated already, and they instantly got up as soon as they have seen him. He waved at everyone and smiled. The President stood in front of the crowd and addressed them.

"Let everyone know those men are sacrificing their lives for the good of mankind. We say thank you and will never forget them," he paused for a while.

"For those who have come back, we say thank you too. To all these brave men and women as the President, I honor them with medals of honor. These medals will remind them of their courage and our gratitude," said the President.

The crowds applauded. The President called names of the returning soldiers one after the other. The soldiers got up and approached the President walking proudly. They saluted the President before he hands them the medals of honor. Everyone clapped hands after they had received a medal. In the seated crowd was a woman and kids. Corporal Hinks's name is called. He stood up and straightened his uniform and walked toward the front with confidence. The people applauded hysterically. Corporal Hinks (former Specialist) smiled and looked over his shoulder. He gave Sergeant Aiden a quick glance. The Sergeant looked back and smiled then applauded. The Corporal stopped at attention in front of the President and saluted.

"Corporal Hinks, I would like to represent the gratitude of the country and award you this medal of honor for acts of courage," said the President putting the medal of honor on the Corporal's neck.

"Thank you, Mr. President," said the Corporal saluting and turning around walking back to his seat. Hysterically the crowd applauded.

A car screeched its tires to a halt outside a house. Dennis got out and walked into the yard of a house. It was night time, and the people were celebrating at Corporal Hinks' house. A large crowd had gathered. Later Corporal Hinks and Sergeant Aiden with their wives were in the lounge having dinner.

"After I got the medal of honor, the nightmares somehow stopped. Isn't that strange?"

said the Corporal astonished.

"It doesn't matter now Corporal. It's in the past now," said the Sergeant.

"There is more to it than meets the eye," replied the Corporal.

"What do you mean?" asked the Sergeant.

"Are you saying we are now protected just because we have been given medals of honor?"

"Even though they can't be sold, Corporal we have achieved something like a status," explained the Sergeant.

In another city Specialist, Kayden aged twenty-six with a crew haircut was watching the game on television. Corporal Hinks entered the lounge with drinks.

"How has it been Specialist?"

"The nightmares. I can't sleep. Deprived of sleep. How did you cope Corporal?"

"We all go through that. Mine were worse especially when I was not in combat," replied the Corporal.

"So, what happened?" asked the Specialist.

The two men briefly watched the game on television.

"After the medal of honor, they stopped, or I got excited and forgot about them. Ever since I have never removed the medal. It's always on me," replied the Corporal.

"What's the catch? Is it like an incentive to keep us fighting in the army? It makes no sense that just because you are awarded the medal of honor then the nightmares stop," said the Sergeant.

"No matter how stupid it sounds that's what happened," replied Corporal Hinks.

The Corporal sipped his drink and sighed.

"I made an oath to serve this country not to be abused by the system. Sleep

deprivation then I can't seem to function after that. A lot of time I am worried about these nightmares," explained the Specialist.

"If you ask me if I would redo this. I would say no," replied the Corporal.

"Why is that? You have everything you love, you love the army, didn't you?" asked Specialist Kayden.

"In my days the army was respected, and soldiers honored. Every time we returned home people greeted us like officials or celebrities. Nowadays they are protests and name-calling," replied the Corporal.

In the city in one hotel Jessica in her thirties with

curly-hair, a brunette was watching the news. The anchorwoman was reading the news.

"Just in a homeless man jumped from the bridge to his death. But an eye witness suggested that he exploded first then fell. His state suggested the eye witness account.

This is one of several accounts of homeless people committing suicides. Aria reporting for Touchladybirdlucky."

Later that day, Jessica was with her friend Gabriela twenty-six a striking blonde girl with hazel eyes.

"Seems humanity is headed for extinction. What did we get us into?" remarked Jessica.

"It seemed like a good idea at first," replied Gabriela.

"Why the suicides?"

"Tough life I guess Jessica," replied Gabriela.

"So, what's with the exploding?"

"That I am not sure maybe let's find out," suggested Gabriela.

A car parked outside the coroner's office and the

two women got out and entered the office, a tiny office with a lot of files and papers on the desk. The interior was averagely decorated. The coroner goes by the name of Banks in his early sixties with gray hair. He looked at the women and pointed at the chairs in front of his desk.

"Let's assume they all were homeless, in that case, there is nothing much we gathered as you all know they all exploded," explained the coroner.

Jessica leaned forward and glanced at Gabriela.

"What if they are not suicides and were detonated?" asked Jessica.

"Coroner said it's likely because the medical device can explode at impact," explained Gabriela.

"But what if someone deliberately detonated them like bombs assuming it's possible," asked Jessica.

A drone passed on top of the two women delivering parcels. Gabriela stopped and looked at the drone.

"Unless if it can be operated like a drone. Bearing in mind the accounts of the eyewitnesses they exploded before impact with the ground. So, you are saying someone is trying to destroy evidence by destroying them? First who would want these men dead and why?" asked Gabriela. She paused and looked at Jessica thinking.

"What do we know about these men?" added Gabriela.

"Gabriela could these be related to the genetic mutations?"

A very large building in the city is well decorated with shining windows. A man walked to the window and looked outside. He noticed a lot of cars and people going their way. He looked further away and dreamed of what might be if he had his way. A knock on the door woke him up from this dream. He walked to his chair and sat down comfortably. The door suddenly opened, and two ladies Gabriela and Jessica walked in.

"What can I do for you ladies?" asked Chunks sitting even more comfortably.

"The men who are committing suicides were they your men? Did they work for you?" asked Jessica with a serious face.

Mr. Chunks smiled and leaned forward.

"Let me see. They were all homeless with no IDs and not paying taxes so definitely not my men. What else?" quipped Mr. Chunks before casting a sarcastic look.

"Who on earth would want these men dead and why?" asked Gabriela.

"You said it yourself that they committed suicides," replied Mr. Chunks trying to be a smart-ass.

"We believe they exploded first. Were these your former subjects?" inquired Jessica.

Mr. Chunks twisted his lips and with a cunning face replied instantly.

"Just speculation."

The two women looked at each other.

"Let me guess. They sued you after your experiments went wrong and then you exploded them to get rid of the evidence," suggested Jessica.

Mr. Chunks touched the table with both his hands and looked at the two ladies.

"Listen ladies you right now you have our instruments protecting you so how come you are not exploding?" he asked.

The two women looked at each other.

"Exactly! These were part of the first-generation experiments when everything was out of control I guess," replied Gabriela.

Mr. Chunks smiled and sat comfortably in his chair.

"Makes no sense we let them live for these years. If we had done something wrong, we could have killed them a long time ago," explained Mr. Chunks.

Jessica got up and walked toward the window. She looked outside and then at Mr. Chunks.

"Maybe they are part of the group that lodged a lawsuit against you so in that case, you can't touch them," suggested Jessica.

Mr. Chunks shook his head.

"Still just speculation," replied Mr. Chunks.

There was a moment of silence. It was Gabriela who broke the ice.

"Or the story is true that the device somehow destroys the person's memory. I read a court case that the device was used to shake the victim's thighs and secretly his brain simultaneously. The man would press down his thighs and the sides of his head," suggested Gabriela.

Mr. Chunks shook his head in disagreement.

"I know. The main reasons you did not worry about them was that you knew they will remember nothing," suggested Jessica.

Mr. Chunks smiled and looked at the ladies.

"Nice try, but not correct."

"Still makes no sense why all now within a short time?"

"Ladies we have a contract with the government these deaths have nothing to do with us," explained Mr. Chunks.

The ladies breathed heavily and stood up to leave. They walked to the door and Jessica turned around and looked at Mr. Chunks.

"One other thing so initially these devices were used for artificial exercising who on earth is that lazy to require your device?"

Mr. Chunks lifted both his hands.

"Can't help," he replied.

"They were not disabled. Who were your first clients?" asked Gabriela.

"Classified," replied Mr. Chunks.

The women left and headed back to their office. They entered their office and Jessica threw her handbag on her desk and slumped in her chair. She looked hopeless and haunted.

"What percentage of people ends up homeless and why?" she asked.

Gabriela quickly typed something on the keyboard.

"People on drugs. But in fact, people on drugs can't be in the streets," she replied.

"Initially it seemed these people were rich. Chunks and his company are crooks. They must have targeted the rich. Destroyed their memory as well during the so-called 'artificial exercise' making them homeless."

"Relatives? They might have told their relatives, so they don't fit the profile. Unless no one else knows. Someone paid for them and asked them to sign a secretive clause?" suggested Gabriela.

The two women through each other a quick glance.

"The army!" they shouted at the same time.

CHAPTER FOUR

In another country, it was night time at a barracks. Inside the tent, Private Kayden was sleeping on the temporary bed. He fidgeted a lot. A close-up revealed his eyes moving under the closed eyelids. He moved his head left then right fast. Sweat bubbles were forming on his forehead. A huge loud-boom-sound shook the ground and woke him up. He picked up his helmet and his rifle and ran outside. A huge blast in front of him saw him flying in the air before landing on the ground. Blood came out of his nose. He slithered on the ground going to the trenches.

Instantly Private Gideon who is twenty-four years old dived next to him.

"Are you hurt Private? Seems you are bleeding," asked Private Gideon.

"I think I will be okay I landed on my face," replied Private Kayden touching his face.

Another night a few weeks later. A cool breeze blew the leaves of the trees and the night creatures sang in the dark forest. Private Gideon was with Private Kayden. They signaled each other before stealthily advancing forward. Voices startled them that they lay on their stomachs. Private Kayden signaled to Private Gideon who then pulled a hand-propelled grenade and loaded it. He kneeled on one knee. He placed the propelled grenade on his shoulder and waited. He threw a glance at Private Kayden.

Private Kayden signaled with his fingers and aimed with a rifle. A whistling sound made them duck and there was a huge boom-sound followed by screams and shouting. The two men then retreated slithering fast. They stopped and threw each other a quick glance.

A car parked in a driveway and Kristi got out of the car carrying her handbag. She looked outside before entering the house. She entered the house and picked up the cat. She opened the cupboard and took out the cat food. She opened the fridge and got out milk and fed the cat. The cat disappeared and scratched the door. Kristi followed the cat before an instant knock at the door startled her. She opened the door and saw two women standing there.

"How can I help you?" asked Kristi.

The two women looked at each other first.

"We understand you registered a missing person and for the reasons which we will explain later we find your case odd and if you don't mind, we would like to ask you some questions," explained Gabriela.

Kristi squinted her eyes for a while and looked at the two women before the cat distracted her.

"Sounds silly I look for the person I buried," Kristi replied walking into the house carrying the cat.

The two women looked at each other. Then followed her inside. They sat on the couch and looked at Kristi. She breathed heavily and cried. The women looked at each other before they tried to console her.

"What seemed to be the problem," asked Jessica. Kristi sobbed for a while.

"All this time I thought he was dead," Kristi replied sobbing.

The two women looked at each other confused.

"Is he not?" asked Jessica before she looked at Gabriela with talking eyes.

"Go on?" insisted Gabriela.

Kristi put the cat down and looked at the two women.

"Weeks ago, I felt things and seeing things I could not explain. I woke up one night, and the window was open. Something quickly jumped outside as the curtain instantly flipped wide-open. I initially thought it was the cat," she paused and looked at the cat.

"Was it not?" asked Gabriela curious.

A moment of silence sliced through the room.

"Not the cat. The cat was under the bed. Then the other night whatever it was

honestly sat on me. I woke up thinking it's the cat. It wasn't. Instantly the curtain flipped wide-open," explained Kristi.

A car entered the research lab yard and parked in the near-full car park. A woman walked to the door. A quick scan and the gate's door opened. She entered inside down the lift and into the research lab. The President, the Professor and the Vice President were in the lab. Kaylee glanced at the President.

"You said you have news for us," said the President.

"The medical device is imitating something. At first, we thought the victim, the man he ran over, but we checked the man's genetic make-up," said the Professor.

"What do we know about the man killed," asked the Vice President.

"A decorated war veteran. Awarded a medal of honor but somehow ended up in the streets," replied Kaylee.

"We think he was under trauma treatment. He had his memory wiped off maybe that went too far," explained Kaylee.

There was a moment of silence before the President broke the ice.

"A war hero. One of my boys. So, I awarded him the medal of honor?" asked the President not expecting an answer.

"Someone or some spirits are inside him," said the Professor.

They all stared at the Professor surprised.

"Yes. The medical device is imitating their DNA make-up clearing all the

abnormalities and genetic disorders," added Kaylee.

"What kind of people are in him?" asked the Vice President not following.

"Women and children," replied Kaylee chillingly.

"Women and children! Oh my God!" shouted the President.

They all looked shocked to hear that.

"Are you saying these souls of women and children were inside the soldier?" asked the President.

"The billionaire accidentally killed the soldier ending up getting the souls of women and children the soldier had killed. The device then imitated their DNA and their genetic make-up clearing all the abnormalities," explained the Professor.

"Mr. President do you know what they are saying?" asked the Vice President.

"Yes exactly," replied the President before continuing.

"Wait, a minute. Did you check the soldier's genetic makeup?"

"Yes, but they have no effect still the device malfunctioned and still caused mutations.

"Are you saying the soldier does not react to the souls?" asked the President.

"Yes, Mr. President. He is just a transporter of souls. He is just a vessel," replied the Professor.

"Are these souls of men as well?" asked the President.

"The genetic make-up means only women and children," replied Kaylee.

"Son of a bitch. I want you to arrest Chunks and close his company," ordered the President angrily.

"Now I understand why he said there was an antidote. This is what he meant. Blood of innocent women and children. This is the language you understand they say seeing is believing," explained the Vice President.

The President walked in the lab pondering all this. He stopped and looked at the Professor and then at Kaylee.

"I am the President of the people, not a blood murderer. I want him arrested," he shouted shaking with anger.

"Now I understand why he kept pushing you to go to war. If he had told you his real motive, he knew you would have refused clever bastard," remarked the Professor.

"He made me betray these men. They put trust in me, and I let them down," explained the President.

"He tricked you. You didn't know. The men will understand," added the Vice

President.

"Son of a bitch. These men took an oath to defend the constitution," said the

President. He paused and looked at everyone.

"I did not send these soldiers to harvest the souls of women and children!" shouted the President.

"Harvesting souls to serve humanity," explained Kaylee.

"The deaths of homeless people are these linked to this as well?" asked the President.

"Yes, I think they were all former soldiers," replied Kaylee.

A woman driving a car stopped her car at the traffic lights and looked at one of the tall buildings. She noticed a man standing at the window in one of the upper-level offices.

The man looked down from the office and saw cars and people minding their businesses. He smiled and looked at the time. He walked back to his seat and sat down. He opened his laptop and smiled. A beep sound went off drawing his attention.

He opened the laptop and looked at the screen. He saw an instant message.

'$10 billion successfully received and transferred to offshore accounts.'

There was an instant knock at the door that seemed to have startled him. Instantly the door opened. Mr. Chunks looked at the door and then saw the President with his bodyguard Zayden who is thirty-four years old with a crew cut hairstyle armed and masculine entering the office.

"Mr. President, what brings you here? Is everything all right?" asked Mr. Chunks worried.

"Let's just say I am visiting an old friend," replied the President.

Mr. Chunks' face changed from sullen to radiant. He felt much relaxed and walked back to his seat.

"Come on in," he told the President and his bodyguard. The door only shut briefly before someone opens it as well. Four men entered the office. These were also the President's bodyguards. Mr. Chunks squinted his eyes and looked at the President.

"You son of a bitch. I am the Chief Commander of my soldiers. Do you know what is trust and loyalty in military circles? It's a bond so strong that you will put your life on it. To make things worse, you let me go to war for the wrong reasons," shouted the President.

"Mr. President, let me explain," said Mr. Chunks.

"Shut up! When I'm talking. Now it makes sense why you told everyone we were going to war to take the oil and resources. You had even worse reasons for waging this war.

Killing women and children that is a crime against humanity," added the President.

"No one can prove that. Only you know. I did this

deliberately, so you know there is a way for all these disorders," replied Mr. Chunks.

The President punched Mr. Chunks heavily that he fell together with his chair.

"Who gave you the right to blow-up my men and kill them like that," asked the President his face creased with rage.

"They made an oath to die for you. To serve their country and that is what is

happening saving humanity from extinction" justified Mr. Chunks.

The President grabbed and lifted Mr. Chunks by his collar and kneed him in the groin. He punched him in the ribs.

"From day one this was a business scheme to you. So, you can steal $ millions from billionaires. In the process you nearly caused the extinction of humanity and dragged me into this, surely I will kill you!" shouted the President angry.

"I saw an opportunity and took it," replied Mr. Chunks.

"Where are your morals? It means you don't respect me. You would rather use me to kill my own men. Why not rob a bank like everyone else? You let me send my men to kill women and children?" remarked the President.

"The souls can reverse everything," explained Mr. Chunks.

"I know you are receiving money for my men after blowing them up. How can you do that? Only you are that evil," questioned the President.

Mr. Chunks wiped the blood from his mouth and cunningly looked at the President.

"Mr. President with all due respect. I helped you," he smiled cheekily.

A jab and a huddle followed by a knee in the ribs made Mr. Chunks growl in pain. Pain exploded within his rib cage as he kneeled touching his rib cage.

Pain he groaned and looked at the President in anger and full of rage.

"You are a warmonger. I did you a favor. I gave you a good reason to go to war," shouted Mr. Chunks.

"Me? A warmonger? A cold-blooded killer? Do cold-blooded killers kill their own men let alone women and kids? I will kill you!" shouted the

President.

"I protected all humanity, and the money is my pay, my reward so I see nothing wrong with that," explained Mr. Chunks.

The President looked at his bodyguard. Mr. Chunks quickly read the message and pleaded with the President.

"No, no, no. Don't kill me the life of the vessels, I mean, the soldiers are in danger," explained Mr. Chunks.

The President raised his hand. Zayden grabbed Mr. Chunks up and gave him a set of punches and kicks. A fist blew him backward. He staggered backward before a series of right and left kicks sends him tumbling to the ground. A lot of pain exploded inside his rib cage. He touched his rib cage and got up. He wiped the blood off his lips. Zayden dragged him up. He lifted his head up just in time to see a knee in his face. He let out a huge groan of pain. Blood rushed out. He wobbled and fell to the floor. Zayden attached a silencer to his gun. Immediately the President walked out leaving Mr. Chunks who raised his hand at him. Zayden frowned at the begging Mr. Chunks and he threw a quick glance with the corner of his eye at the President. The President walked outside the office with the rest of the bodyguards. Zayden frowned and aimed at Mr.

Chunk before he embedded a bullet in Mr. Chunks' head. He soon after left the office. The Specialist, Kayden is in his house when he suddenly woke up in pain. The Specialist held his thighs and pressed them hard against his leg bone. He felt his calves vibrating. Instantly he touched the side of his head. He dwindled to the window and squinted his eyes and glanced outside. He stood there for a while before he had a flashback. In the flashback, the young private Kayden raised his right hand. In the flashback he was at the army barracks giving the oath of enlistment.

"I Private Kayden do solemnly swear that I will support and defend...," remembered Kayden making an oath of enlistment on his special day in the army.

In another city, a car parked next to another car. its night time and cigarette smoke came out from the window. The man from one car jumped out of his car and into the other.

"The nightmares again?" asked the Corporal.

"Voices of women and kids. Filled my head. I thought I am losing it," replied the Specialist.

"We all go through that. A way to keep us fighting. When you are not there it's these nightmares," replied the Corporal.

"I went shopping a few days ago. This young baby stared at me. I felt like something jumped out of my body. My body pressure subdued," explained the Specialist.

"Go on," requested the Corporal.

"The baby crawled in front of me and touched the air giggling, crawling and running away as if playing with some other invisible baby. Everyone shocked and surprised looked at the baby as he played," explained the Specialist.

The Corporal looked at the Specialist and squinted his eyes.

"What are you saying, Specialist?"

The Specialist breathed and looked outside the car for a while. He puffed his cigarette and replied.

"A soldier appeared behind the boy. The boy got up. He looked at me and stretched his arm as if motioning. He signaled and called me moving his fingers. He cried and walked toward me. He came near my sullen face. I felt this pressure pain in my body.

The baby cried.

Corporal Hinks nodded his head. The Specialist paused and looked away first. He then glanced at the Corporal and opened his eyes.

"Corporal what are we?" he asked and remained gazed at the Corporal expecting an instant answer.

The Corporal took his time thinking. He puffed his cigarette and replied.

"Soldiers Specialist Kayden. Soldiers," he explained.

"The other day a woman sat next to me. She said oops you got a lot of demons. She paused and pondered for a while then she asked me if I was a soldier?"

"The war is ending," said the Corporal.

"There is no more war. Everyone has come back home. My questions are what we are?"

"Soldiers the best honorable men out there," replied the Corporal.

The two men looked at each other. Silence broke out for a while.

"Admit it, Corporal, we are bloody transporters of souls. We are bloody women and kids' soul smugglers," remarked the Specialist.

The Corporal looked angrily.

"What got into you to think like that? Like I said we are honorable soldiers," explained the Corporal.

The Specialist smiled and looked at the Corporal.

"Nothing but just soul smugglers," added the Specialist.

The Corporal punched the Specialist very hard.

"Behave, soldier. I am an honorable man so as you and we took an oath to defend this country. No better men of principle than us!" shouted the Corporal.

Specialist Kayden rubbed blood from his split lip.

"Yes, Sir if you think so Corporal but I am afraid you are in the dark even worse than me," cunningly replied the Specialist.

"Behave, soldier. You are just upset. You think I will go to war so I can be a vessel for the souls of women and kids. How can you say that?" questioned the Corporal.

"No, sir. We are men of honor, loyalty and trust are within our bones. I am afraid we have been betrayed. The President betrayed us," added the Specialist.

"Maybe you should see a shrink!" shouted the Corporal.

The Specialist pushed the idea aside and cunningly smiled.

"You know they double-crossed us. We are just a bunch of soul hunters, soul

collectors, soul transporters, you name it," explained the Specialist.

The Corporal's face changed instantly it seemed a ball of pain exploded within

himself. His face creased with rage. He shook with anger. He got out of the car and walked in front of the car. He opened the other door and grabbed the Specialist out of the car. He kneed him in the ribs and punched him in the face.

"Maybe I take out for you these demons in your head soldier!" shouted the Corporal. Specialist Kayden laughed as he nursed his rib cage and his lips.

"You know why your nightmares stopped? Do you?" asked the Specialist laughing and groaning in pain at the same time.

The Corporal's face was covered with anger.

"Say it!" he shouted.

The Specialist laughed.

"They groomed you like chicken. Now you are ready to be harvested. The medal is like a watermark. A seal that no `one takes you until your buyer, some crazy, rich billionaire comes to buy you," scorned the Specialist.

The Corporal on hearing this lost it and lunged aggressively. He threw a series of punches and kicks fiercely only stopping when the Specialist wobbled and fell to the ground. He groaned as pain detonated inside his rib cage. He sat and looked at the Corporal. He wiped blood from his nose.

"It does not stop there," added the Specialist taunting the Corporal.

The Corporal raised his leg to throw a kick, but he didn't.

"Maybe I kill you myself," he added.

"Listen to this. This is the interesting part. For the billionaire buyer to take out his souls of which you are carrying, he must kill you first," the Specialist burst into laughter.

The Corporal squinted his eyes and sat down next to the Specialist.

"I suspected it, Specialist. Look, stupid me, taking it on you. I apologize. I am like a sitting duck. Betrayed all these years," explained the Corporal.

The two men looked at each other.

"They created electronic-viruses that fly in the air and using these medical devices which were presumed to protect us then search for rich millionaires.

The Corporal looked lost.

"And then?" he asked.

"The viruses then link us and synchronize our movements so that we will meet so that somehow the buyer can collect his souls of women and children. The medical device has a digital electronic number unique to you, a serial number which they used to locate and link you with the soul buyer," explained the Specialist.

"Meaning?"

The Specialist took his breath and continued.

"Whoever buys that medal knows exactly where you are through satellite positioning,"

replied the Specialist.

The Corporal looked scared and looked around.

"So, what's wrong with these billionaires why they need me? I mean the souls we do carry?" asked the Corporal.

"It's a big billion-dollar business. The health bill made it compulsory for the

government to insist that everyone must have this medical device initially to protect us but it's coming to light they had more sinister motives,' added the Specialist.

The two men looked at each other.

"Funny they said it was for artificial exercising when we were in combat," quipped the Corporal.

"They use this to wipe out your memory too like a nightmare therapy when they are the ones depriving you of sleep this is just plain stupid if not mere evil. Isn't this torture?"

"Is this why decorated soldiers end up in the streets? What do these souls do for these billionaires?" asked the Corporal.

The Specialist looked saddened.

"The device caused mutations weakening humans, creating a range of genetic disorders. Somehow these souls reverse the side effects, remember these are souls of pure women and children from areas less affected by the use of these medical devices.

I guess that's why they send us to wars in other less developed countries," explained the Specialist.

"These bastards destroying mankind. Those days abroad they used to call us soul harvesters we thought it's because they thought we went to war to steal resources, oil and the like," explained the Corporal.

"Yes, oil but meaning 'oil for these devices', in the form of women and children souls," replied the Specialist.

There was a moment of silence.

"I pray that the President is not involved in this," said the Corporal.

"I feel the same way too," remarked the Specialist.

"So, if we have these souls why the genetic mutations don't change in soldiers?" asked the Corporal.

"They created a virus they call a blocker. Remember all the immunization jabs at the beginning of combat? The device acts like a CD player. It must be loaded to play the music, in this case, the viruses," added the Specialist.

"So, some soldiers consume souls?"

"It's like a Yardi smoking his stash surely his boss won't be pleased with him. That's why they blow them up like bombs," replied the Specialist.

"That explains the homeless people of which most are former soldiers who are being found dead blown up to pieces? Jesus!" shouted the Corporal.

The two men laughed sat in the car park.

Inside a huge office building in the city, the two ladies were in the office.

"Speaking of evil people. Just imagine these soldiers were sent to war to kill women and children just to cover for the side effects of these medical devices," said Jessica sitting down.

"Chunks company tricked the government so that the government cleans its mess," replied Gabriela.

"They are not side effects. They created viruses and deliberately caused these diseases, so they extort money from the millionaires and demand huge budgets.

"Would that not fall under crimes against humanity?"

CHAPTER FIVE

The Corporal wore his uniform and his medal of honor. He looked at himself in the mirror. He saluted and opened a small box. He took something and quickly shoved it in his pocket. He stood in his bedroom before getting into his car. He drove his car to the city. The car stopped on the traffic lights. There were kids playing not far away from the traffic light on the other side of the fence. The Corporal looked at the kids playing. The kids instantly stopped playing and looked in his direction. The kids ran away. One of them fell and screamed. The sound of the horn being blasted from the car behind startled him he drove off fast. In the city, the Corporal knocked briefly at the open door and entered inside the office. The office was well decorated. The comfort of the carpet as he stepped in said it all. This was not just an office. This was the luxurious Office of the President. He instantly heard running water in the bathroom. The President was in the bathroom. The door of the bathroom was slightly opened. The Corporal could hear water running out of the tape. The Corporal looked around before a beep sound startled him. He looked where the sound came from. There was a laptop on the desk. He moved closer and looked at the screen and read the message.

'Money just received $1 billion for medal 2102,'

This was the message displayed on the screen. Astonished the Corporal looked closely.

He leaned forward. He had a close-up look at the message. Instantly his heartbeat jumped high. Inside the bathroom, the President was washing his hands.

"We need to push harder with the medals. I took care of Mr. Chunks," said the

President in the bathroom enough for the Corporal to have heard.

The Corporal looked around instinctively wondering to whom the President was talking to. The President came out rubbing his hands with a hand towel looking down. He lifted his head and his eyes came face to face with the Corporals. He quickly glanced at the Corporal and instantly at the computer screen. He looked at the Corporal's face and noticed that something was wrong. He quickly walked to the laptop and pushed the side panel down closing it.

"Where is the Vice President?" asked the President looking around.

"That's my medal number. $1 billion for what?" asked the Corporal seriously ignoring the President's question. The President paused for a while. He looked at Corporal Hinks straight in his eyes.

"It's not what it seems soldier," said the President.

The Corporal pulled out the gun and pointed at the President. The President did not look alarmed at all.

"You lied to us, how could you? We are men of honor. You betrayed us. We trusted you, but you turned us into murderers, even worse making us women and children killers," remarked the Corporal.

There was a moment of silence.

"Just think about the oath soldier. The oath to obey the President. Put the gun down Soldier.

"You sold me? I saw my medal number," asked the Corporal.

The President looked at the closed laptop not

knowing what to say.

"Like I said soldier it's not what it seems. I am on your side soldier," replied the President.

The Corporal lifted the gun before the bullet sound rocketed in the building.

A few moments later in the President's office Specialist, Kayden was standing in the room. The Corporal was on the floor shot in the stomach. He was lying down with blood covering his hands.

"Specialist Kayden what did you do that for?" asked the Corporal still lying on the ground with a gun on the floor beside him.

"The nightmares. He said he can make them stop. I took an oath to protect him remember?" replied the Specialist.

The President was standing near his desk. He looked at the Corporal and then the Specialist and smiled. He stretched his hand.

"Give me your gun Specialist," requested the President.

The Corporal looked scared and looked at the Specialist.

"Don't give him the gun. He has already sold my medal!" shouted the Corporal.

Specialist Kayden handed the gun to the President.

"Go on Soldier. Take his gun and finish him that's an order."

Specialist Kayden walked toward the Corporal who was on the floor and picked his gun next to him. He looked at the President with the Corporal's gun in his hand.

"I took an oath to protect the President," said the Specialist before pausing.

He aimed the gun at the Corporal.

"And to obey his orders," said the Corporal.

The Corporal lifted his head.

"He will kill you too Specialist!" shouted the Corporal.

The Specialist pulled the trigger. A car suddenly screeched its tires to a halt outside the President's office. A bodyguard jumped out before he heard another gunshot sound. He pulled his gun and ran to the door. He pushed the door.

It's night time in one city. Olivia was watching the television. In the news an

anchorwoman was reading the news. Mr. Chunks was shot dead by Corporal Hinks and Specialist Kayden who were shot dead by Chunks' bodyguards before the bodyguards were arrested. This comes in the wake of Chunks Ltd being sued by people around the world after a series of genetic disorders and mutations caused by the medical device. The court cases will financially cripple Chunks Ltd."

CHAPTER SIX

Seventeen years later. After the wars, the oil burned in the air after the sabotage attacks. This resulted in air pollution for some time and this increased the demand and need for sophisticated medical devices to help clean the air before the air is absorbed in the body. With these comes other unforeseen problems, or let's say business opportunities for the cold-blooded. A receptionist at one hotel was sitting in her chair listening to the voice over on the radio.

'After the world, human rights wars claimed many lives the seven most developed countries after being defeated and marginalized formed a pact. These seven countries became one and known as the territory of the Riches and Prosperity. The rest of the world become known as the Territory of Carolinadeivid even though countries had their own governments. The most profitable five-coastal countries were now under the territory of Carolinadeivid. This territory controlled most of the trade routes and most of the oil-producing regions.

After the wars oil had become scarce and expensive outside Carolinadeivid territory. Carolinadeivid territory controlled all the natural resources mainly oil whereas the territory of Riches and Prosperity controlled software and business. In one city Kaylynn, a thirty-six-year-old with a striking blonde hair and close-set deep blue eyes with a pronounced face and cheeks is with Hayden. A forty-year-old man with a masculine body shape and taper fade hair. These two were now the leaders of the territory of Riches and Prosperity even though the other countries had their own leaders. The other leaders were all subordinates to them.

"I think we should go on with the plan," said Kaylynn.

Hayden kept silent for a while thinking. He lifted his head and looked at her.

"Willing to take that risk?" he asked.

Instantly Kaylynn replied with much confidence.

"What other option do we have? This is the only option," she explained.

Hayden stood up and breathed heavily.

"Send them," ordered Kaylynn.

On the other side of the world in the Carolinadeivid territory. Cayden twenty-eight years old and masculine with a crew cut hairstyle and hooded eyes was in the office. A brunette aged thirty-two-years-old and a curvy lady walked in. Cayden touched his forehead as if in pain.

"What's wrong with the system?" he asked looking at Kaydence. He quickly dragged his chair close to the screen in front of him. He typed quickly frequently touching his forehead.

"Not sure but I am receiving stress signals. See if you can pinpoint from where

exactly," said Kaydence.

"Trace the signal from within our territory I will trace it from outside," suggested Cayden.

They both touched their foreheads frequently entering information on the computers.

A few seconds later they had clasped hands looking at each other. A beep sound instantly came from the computer speakers on the screen.

"Come on! Show the location," shouted Cayden. A circle formed on the screen. The circle rotated for a while before two arrows approached each other and joined. Instantly a flag was inserted on the map. The couple threw each other a quick glance.

"This is the tower we have intrusion, or a security alert please send back-up at the following coordinates ...," said Cayden into the radio system.

In one city, a group of men were at their post outside a building. A crackling sound on the talking radios startled them. Soon after some men dispersed. Among them was Donovan a twenty-eight-year-old with a crew cut and armed. Jasper twenty-nine old of average-built loaded too. The third man was Ryker a twenty-eight-year-old man of medium build and lastly was Brycen a twenty-nine-year-old masculine man who happened to be armed as well. The men instantly jumped into the patrol SUV.

"Go! Go! Go! Go, drive!!" shouted Brycen the leader of the group.

The car traveled quick passing other cars before stopping miles away. The men got off and pointed guns as they arrived at a building. Signaling directions at each other they entered the building. Stealthily with raised guns, they scanned the building. Ryker stopped and looked at the other men.

"Oh my God! What happened here?" he asked

looking ahead of him.

Donovan quickly looked at Ryker and radioed the headquarters.

"Headquarters we need back-up as soon as possible," requested Donovan. A cracking sound was heard instantly.

"What happened what is the state of your emergency?"

"We need back-up a lot of casualties. Send emergence vans," requested Donovan.

People lay on the ground. The men ran around checking if some people were still alive. Some had already died.

There was a huge tower near the coast. Inside the tower was Cayden and Kaydence.

Cayden stared at the screen and then at Kaydence.

"What happened out there? Find out, will you?" said Kaydence looking worried.

"This is the tower do you copy?"

"Loud and clear. A lot of casualties. We sent back-up already," replied the tower on the radio.

"I want an estimate! quickly!" shouted Cayden his voice showing enormous stress patterns.

"I don't know the figures," replied the headquarters' operator over the radio.

"Connect me with the back-up team as soon as possible requested Cayden.

Cayden stood up and paced in the tower.

Over the other side of the tower, a crackling sound on the radio startled everyone in the building. Jasper quickly answered the radio.

"Receiving loud and clear," he replied.

"Quickly count how many people have died and how many are alive and what's their status," requested Cayden over the radio.

"Over twenty casualties and some alive upstairs," replied Jasper.

Cayden stopped and touched his forehead. Then entered the figures.

"Touch one of the deceased on the forehead and send me the details hurry," requested Cayden.

Jasper touched the forehead of one victim and touched himself on the forehead.

The tower was a big oval building overlooking the border and the sea. Over the past months, Cayden and Kaydence had been the main occupants. The tower had big screens and the view outside was spectacular. Inside Cayden and Kaydence had received stress signals and all the warning lights and call for help indicators were on.

The two looked at each other for a while. The computer beeped a sound and Cayden sat down quickly.

"Come on," he shouted looking at the screen. An alert beep went off and a flashing radiating circle appeared on the screen.

"Damn it! Oh my God. Quickly radio headquarters raise the alarm!" shouted Cayden.

He paused and continued.

" Level 7!"

"Level 7? Where are they?" asked Kaydence.

"Within the danger zone. Hurry!"

"This is the tower. It's an emergency evacuate

everyone straight away raise the alarm category 7. I repeat level 7," repeated Kaydence.

"This is the tower evacuate immediately you have less than 5 minutes or perish there.

I repeat evacuate," Kaydence.

"What? We have already called for backup. Some people are still alive," replied Jasper.

"What did he say! Tower what's the status?" asked Brycen.

Cayden remained silent. He stared at Kaydence and pointed to the screen. Kaydence instantly got up and removed the headphones. A voice becomes audible. That went on for some time before anyone answered. Then Cayden answered.

"This is the tower," he paused.

"Yes, go on. We can hear you," replied Brycen.

"Tower are you receiving? We are waiting for backup. What is the status?" requested Brycen.

"You know the drill. Let's go there is nothing you can do. Let's evacuate!" shouted Kaydence.

The atmosphere in the building was that of fear

and confusion. Brycen did his best to avoid panicking. He knew time was running out, and he knew what their orders were. There were many people whose lives were at risk. This was not just about saving his ass. There was a lot of weight on his shoulders. Brycen and Jasper simultaneously radioed the tower with no luck. Cayden took a deep breath and placed the radio closer.

"This is the tower," said Cayden.

"Yes, go ahead!" replied Brycen.

"I am sorry it's not a 7 it's a 10," said Cayden on the radio.

Instantly silence broke out. The men looked at each other.

"What! You said a 7! Why you called for backup if it was a 10?" shouted Brycen.

"I sincerely apologize. Good luck," said Cayden.

"Son of a bitch! It's a 10!" shouted Jasper.

All the men stared at each other.

The alarms in the tower had already sounded. The warning lights had already flashed. The atmosphere had become serious. Kaydence left the tower. Cayden received more stress signals. Alarms were buzzing with calls for help from all over.

"Damn it. Kaydence! Come back!" shouted Cayden. He ran outside shouting.

"Kaydence! Come back!"

"No, we must evacuate!" shouted Kaydence.

"We have more stress signals!"

Kaydence stopped instantly.

"What? Are you sure?" she paused.

"Oh God we will die!" shouted Kaydence.

Hesitantly she ran back upstairs.

"What is the problem? We can't stay here. We must evacuate."

Cayden quickly entered the information in the computer.

"All five-coastal areas wiped out? So, there is no point. Let's go then." shouted Kaydence.

"We can only go if we are sure that there is nothing we can do."

"Oh my God, all five? Impossible!" shouted Kaydence.

CHAPTER SEVEN

On the other side of the city Dakota now forty-four years old a masculine man with short volumized hair was the overseer of the territory of Carolinadeivid. A siren startled him. He glanced at the screen and quickly called Layleen who was twenty- seven years old with ginger hair of slim built but tall. She was also his wife.

"Level 8! Run to the bunker quickly!" shouted Dakota to his wife.

Layleen ran out and entered the elevators followed by Dakota. Several other men were already inside.

"Tower are you receiving? This is the overseer. I repeat tower are you receiving?" radioed Dakota.

Over the other side in the tower the situation was critical. The siren has been on for some time now. The lights on the screen had turned red from amber. The tower was jammed with calls for help and there was not much they can do. Cayden got up and looked at the big screen. He paced in the tower. Kaydence looked at him her heartbeat highly elevated. Kaydence's face suddenly became sullen. She threw a quick look at Cayden.

"Don't answer. If you answer we are all dead!" shouted Kaydence.

Cayden looked lost for a minute or two.

"We can't abandon the tower," explained Cayden.

"Let's go I don't want to die! Come Cayden!" shouted Kaydence walking out of the tower room. Cayden stared at her and took a deep breath.

"Activate the bunker let's go!" said Kaydence.

"I will activate the bunker for you close it from the inside. Ok?" shouted Cayden.

He looked at her as she stopped and looked back at him.

"Go ahead! I will be with you," said Cayden but not convincing enough. His voice patterns revealed that he was stressed and not telling the truth of which she instantly sensed this.

"Liar! You are not coming. I know the drill last man standing the man in the tower!" she shouted.

In the city, most of the people had run into the bunkers among them Dakota who waited and radioed the tower again.

"Yes, sir. It doesn't look good. Three already are level ten category." replied Cayden on the radio.

"Is it an attack? All five that's impossible?" shouted Dakota on the radio.

Cayden took the time to reply. A cracking sound startled Dakota.

"Friendly! It seems to radiate from within."

There was a moment of silence. Dakota looked shocked and scared.

"That can't be right. Check again. Will you?" requested Dakota.

A moment of silence before a cracking voice became audible.

"Affirmative."

Dakota kept silent and paced in the bunker.

"Give me a profile?"

Cayden retrieved information from the computer. He was breathing heavily. He looked at the screen before a voice-over startled him. He listened. It was Kaydence checking how long before he goes to the bunker, but he did not reply.

"Subjects all under thirty," said Cayden.

Dakota cast an agonized look. He looked at his wife. She could read from his face that something was wrong. He tried to hide it. Layleen moved closer and hugged him tightly.

"What is it darling you look like you have seen a ghost?" asked Layleen.

Dakota did not say a thing he stared at Layleen. A cracking voice on the radio startled both.

"Dakota are you still there! Dakota are you receiving?" asked Cayden.

Dakota breathed heavily and moved away from Layleen before he answered.

"Loud and clear," he replied.

He looked at Layleen and felt a sad feeling.

"Sorry to tell you this but Layleen has the same batch number. Let her out of the bunker."

Dakota placed the radio down and looked at Layleen.

"What is it darling? Why do you look at me like that?" she sobbed.

In the tower, Cayden stood up and walked toward the window. He looked outside. The coastal area had been deserted. He could see the reflection of the warning lights above the tower in the side windows of the tower. He breathed heavily and thought about Kaydence who was already in the bunker. He walked to the desk and sat down. He looked at the screen in front of him and a tear dropped. Instantly the elevator doors suddenly opened. Kaydence appeared at the door and she ran back into the tower.

Cayden shocked and surprised got up.

"Why have you come back? I told you to lock the bunker from inside. I am not going with you! I can't leave the tower. You know?" explained Cayden.

"Don't shout! I love you. Come with me. Abandon the tower. Someone has just

radioed that they have started exploding. Come with me. Come Cayden. I am not leaving you here. Save yourself," pleaded Kaydence.

A beep sound startled both. Instantly a countdown timer began. Kaydence walked toward the flashing screen. She looked at the screen.

"Oh my God! Who on earth would do that? That's so evil!" she shouted.

Cayden looked down and hugged her. He snogged her for a while with their foreheads in contact with each other.

"Layleen!" she paused and looked at Cayden.

"Does the overseer know?" asked Kaydence with eyes covered in tears.

Cayden nodded in agreement.

In another city, the back-up team was in the building after being sent to rescue the people. The team comprised Brycen, Jasper, Donovan, and Ryker. The men were in the building with the dead and the other people who were still alive but requiring medical attention.

"Damn it. It's all our generation!" shouted Brycen.

"What are you saying?" asked Ryker.

"What do you think? They sent us to die here,"

added Brycen.

"You saying the Headquarters sent us here to die? Do they know?" asked Donovan.

The men looked at each other contemplating all this.

"Don't play games," said Jasper.

"I checked everyone here they are all under thirty-years-old," replied Brycen.

The men looked at Brycen.

"Meaning?" asked Ryker.

"I checked those who have died all of them are under thirty-years-old and below twenty-seven years old. All those still alive like us are above twenty-seven years but below thirty," explained Brycen.

Ryker looked confused and looked at Brycen.

"So?" asked Ryker.

"All the dead have the same immunization batch number," replied Brycen.

A moment of silence that was short-lived passed as

the radio cracked as Jasper listened.

"So, are you saying this is an inside job? Who is doing this?" asked Donovan.

"The previous government, before the war they immunized everyone. They made it compulsory," replied Brycen.

Jasper paced up and down the room.

"Are you saying the previous government deliberately laced immunization jabs so they can wipe out an entire generation? That's evil. I don't believe you," he added.

"The tower said there was an attack?" asked Donovan.

"Attack just to kill only people of the same age? I don't think so, this is more than just an attack," explained Jasper.

"What are we waiting for? Let's go if it's an inside job then let's fight this," said Ryker.

"You don't get it. If you go out there, you will explode. The area is marked already," explained Brycen.

"So, you say that the previous government laced

their own people with what? Who would do that?" asked Jason.

"They did not know, I guess. They had vaccines deals in exchange for resources, oil, and diamonds. I think they did not know that this would come to this. I think the real question is who supplied them with these vaccines?" explained Jasper.

"These five-coastal areas were the most profitable. This was first implemented as a population control, but no one knew that. So, does that mean someone was milking these areas and creating a time bomb as well?" asked Brycen.

"So, are we going to die here?" asked Ryker.

"He said we wait for the back-up we radioed for," replied Brycen.

"What exactly did he say?" asked Jasper.

Brycen took a long breath.

"He said to wait for the back-up and good luck," replied Brycen looking outside the window.

Ryker looked astonished and terrified.

"Code name for death! I am going out. I am not waiting to be blown up here?" shouted Ryker.

Ryker picked up his gun and sprinted outside. Brycen sprinted after him. He lunged and grabbed him. The two men tumbled onto the floor.

"Don't go they will blow you up," shouted Brycen.

"Let me go! Either way, we will die!" shouted Ryker.

The other men looked at each other.

"Do you hear any sirens? So, we can make it. Stay put, OK?" explained Brycen.

Ryker lunged at Brycen and punched him in the face. He kicked him in the ribs. He sprinted away but Brycen got up and chased after him tripping him to the ground.

The men exchanged punches.

"I am your leader. Wait inside or you will activate the sirens and get everyone blown up. There are sensors at the door. See?" Brycen explained pointing at the side of the door.

"I have to go. The corpse will explode first. Either way, we are toast. I bet. I will take my chances. So, let me go." shouted Ryker.

Brycen kicked him to the ground and sat on him pinning him to the ground.

Somehow, he hooked Brycen's neck with his legs and slammed him to the ground.

Ryker got up and pointed the gun at him. The other men tried to stop him, but he pointed the gun at them too.

"Don't even think about it?" shouted Ryker pointing a gun at everyone.

The automatic doors instantly opened. Ryker stepped outside and jumped into the car. He quickly changed gears and drove away from the building screeching the car's tires. He drove as fast as he can. He looked in the rear-view mirror. A huge fireball engulfed the building as an explosion shattered the building and the cars' windows. He looked in the rear-view mirror and cursed but delighted that he had made the right decision. Instantly a beep sound went off in the car and he looked around to check what it was.

"Oh no!" he shouted and looked like he had seen a ghost.

The car exploded instantly. The ground shook that the tremors were felt miles away even in the tower. In the other territory of the Riches and

Prosperity, it was life as normal. In a huge house, Kaylynn and Hayden had just finished having sex, and they lay on the bed.

"We can take back what is ours. We can be rich again," said Kaylynn.

"I got the feeling that Dakota somehow will survive this," suggested Hayden.

Kaylynn got up and sat down frowning.

"How can he survive this? Layleen remember? Did you do like I said?" asked Kaylynn.

Hayden looked lost for a second before he nodded in agreement.

"I don't know how just a gut feeling. How many times has he escaped your plots?" asked Hayden.

"By tomorrow all that will be ours. All the five-coastal areas. I told you I will never beg for oil. By tomorrow everything will be okay," said Kaylynn.

"Wait a minute, are you telling me you are detonating everyone, I mean every batch," asked Hayden in shock. Kaylynn cunningly smiled and got up and walked into the bedroom.

"Those who are left, will all run away. Leave some

under twenty-sevens intact these will rot there and drive everyone away. The rest boom- they will all explode. We will have our land again," added Kaylynn.

"I never understood you. We have everything we need here you didn't have to do that," advised Hayden.

Kaylynn walked toward Hayden fuming with rage.

"How can you say that? You forgot already? Just seventeen years ago they nearly killed us all. We had to run from the coastal areas. By tomorrow we get back our coastal areas and all the oil will be our gain," explained Kaylynn.

In the other territory. The situation is now very critical in the tower. Cayden got up and walked to the window, tears down his cheeks. The huge explosion startled him as the tower shook. He looked outside through the window. It was like the end of the world. A lot of buildings were on fire with smoke coming from everywhere. He cried and looked at his watch. He pulled a gun and touched his head with it. Instantly a beep sound came from the tower computer. He ran to check what that was. He briefly smiled when he saw where the message had come from.

Message on the screen.

It's Dakota how many minutes do we have?

Quickly he grabbed a chair and sat down.

"Dakota it's the tower are you receiving!" shouted Cayden.

There was silence for a while. A cracking sound sends a shivering feeling of relief and hope.

"Receiving loud and clear. How much time do we have? Are you sure it's this batch only?" asked Dakota.

There was a moment of silence.

"Layleen. OK wait a minute," replied Cayden.

Cayden entered the information in the computer. He looked at the information.

"Quickly give me Layleen's date of birth. I repeat quickly give me Layleen's date of birth we have little time left!" shouted Cayden on the radio.

"It's too late we left the bunker the two of us," said Dakota sad and hopeless.

Instantly Cayden replied.

"You can't do that? Save yourself first. You are the overseer of the people. If you die, we will all perish," he paused and listened.

"If I die. I will save all of you because there won't be any war after that," replied

Dakota tearful.

Silence broke out.

"Somehow, they activated all the batches except yours," advised Cayden.

"Why? Let me see," replied Dakota. There was a moment of silence while he pondered what all this means.

"What are you suggesting?" he added.

"I was thinking of isolating Layleen's batch number, so she won't explode after she dies. That way you will survive but, you must be in the bunker yourself. Go back in the bunker now," advised Cayden.

Dakota felt like crying. He realized what was going on.

"Clever manipulating bitch," he whispered but loud enough for Cayden to have heard.

"Excuse me! What?" asked Cayden.

Dakota thought for a while.

"I got it!" he shouted.

"Go ahead I am listening," said Cayden.

"Kaylynn is using Layleen as a bomb. She is not trying to spare my life. I think she knew you being you, you will check and find out that she hasn't activated my batch. That way gives me a sense of security while Layleen awaits to do her dirty work," replied Dakota.

"I never thought of it that way. I see that makes sense," replied Cayden.

"I think she figured out I would never leave her," added Dakota.

"OK quickly give me Layleen's date of birth. I will try to isolate this. The system is already open as some batch numbers have already exploded," asked Cayden.

Dakota's face became radiant for a minute or two. Cayden frantically entered functions after functions into the computer. He sweated as sweat droplets formed on his forehead. He typed quickly on the keyboard frequently checking the time. Cayden said something to Dakota over the radio, but Dakota was miles away imagining what the future meant. He answered Cayden and listened. He shook his head.

"What? No, I can't do that," replied Dakota.

"Listen that's your only chance now. No time to go to the bunker. Quickly you know the drill," pleaded Cayden.

CHAPTER EIGHT

In another city, all the people were now in the bunkers and only Dakota and his wife Layleen were outside. Dakota stared at Layleen. She looked back at him like she had seen a ghost. Dakota kissed her and asked her to close her eyes. A huge thump was heard as she slumped to the ground. Instantly a huge explosion was heard on the radio. Dakota stopped and looked around only to be startled by the cracking sound of the radio.

"Dakota, are you receiving? Dakota are you still there?" shouted Cayden on the radio.

In the tower above Cayden was busy trying what he can to save Dakota the overseer of the people. Kaydence was in the bunker underneath the tower. She paced left and right as she listened to all the calls for help on the radio. A huge explosion shook the roof of the bunker that bad that she slumped down. She wept like a baby as dust-covered her. On the other side of the world in a different territory. Hayden and Kaylynn were talking together. Kaylynn got up and walked to the big screen.

"Get the antidote darling tomorrow we will send our men first to secure the five-coastal areas. First, we secure our coastal borders. The money we have collected will be like protection money. We will establish a new territory, and everyone shall pay protection money to us," explained Kaylynn.

In the other territory in one bunker Keyon, a thirty-three-year-old heavily masculine and handsome man with dimples on the chin and cheeks looked at his watch. He looked around at everyone. In their previous drills, normally, the overseer would address the people, but Dakota had other issues to worry about everyone. He was gone. Keyon looked at everyone and gathered them around.

"If I don't get back in ten minutes lock the bunker from inside okay?" Shortly after that Keyon got into the elevator and was taken up.

Just outside the bunker Layleen and Dakota were lying on the floor. Layleen was bleeding heavily. Keyon kneeled and checked her pulse. He stopped the bleeding. He lifted her up and into the elevator he went carrying her. Dakota was injured from the blast and window fragments had caused an injury to him. Keyon minutes later return and took Dakota downstairs into the bunker. Inside the bunker, Keyon and the others were nursing Dakota and Layleen's wounds when Keyon looked at everyone and spoke to them.

"I think they are all going to be okay. Layleen has stopped bleeding, but she is still unconscious. Dakota was fast asleep but alive," he advised the people. Later Dakota woke up and helped Keyon nursing his wife. He smiled to find everyone

surrounding them. He frowned a little.

"She has lost a lot of blood," advised Keyon.

"How bad?" asked Dakota.

"Not sure but I don't think it's life-threatening but having said that I think we are running out of time," added Keyon.

Dakota touched his wounds and got up.

"How are you anywhere? She will be okay; she needs a blood transfusion."

"She has been through a lot of maybes good idea to let her sleep for a while," said Dakota.

"Just in time. I understand the system is open now," said Keyon walking to the bunkers' computer.

"She was watermarked. I removed the bomb, and that's the explosion that knocked us down. The bomb exploded seconds after removing it. I hope she will be okay," explained Dakota.

Dakota limped forward in front of everyone. He addressed everyone. They all asked questions most of which he had answers to, but he did not understand what the main reason for the attack was. Or why now after all these years? Surely Kaylynn had something in store for them sure to exterminate the whole population. It was in the middle of the meeting that a beep sound went off loud enough to be heard by everyone. They all stopped and looked at Dakota. For a split-second silence sliced through the bunker. They all looked at Layleen who lay peacefully.

"What was that?" asked Nancy.

"I thought you said you removed the bobby-trap?" inquired Keyon.

Everyone looked at Dakota who looked confused himself.

"Yes? What is it?" questioned Keyon. Dakota breathed heavily and looked at Keyon straight in the eyes.

"Yes, I am sure I removed it," insisted Dakota.

"So, if you removed it then what is that?"

"I am not sure of myself. I think we need privacy. Let's find out," said Dakota.

Keyon and Dakota were in the private room with Layleen. They were examining her.

Layleen was lying on the bed fast asleep peacefully like a baby. Another beep startled the two men. They looked at each other. The sound came straight from her. Dakota quickly kneeled by her side and ogled her for a split-second before he investigated.

"They must have given her two booby traps?" suggested Keyon.

"How can she have two? That's impossible," replied Dakota.

"I don't know. Unless...," said Keyon without finishing his sentence.

Dakota signaled Keyon to follow him and the two entered the spare room in the bunker.

"What are your thoughts?" asked Keyon.

Dakota breathed heavily and stopped pacing. He looked at Keyon.

"We have to operate on her again," replied Dakota.

Keyon got up and paced in the other room in the bunker.

"Damn it! It's Kaylynn," said Dakota.

"What do you mean?" asked Keyon.

"She knew I love her and that I would not let her die," replied Dakota.

"Are you saying the first one was just a decoy?" asked Keyon afraid at the thought.

"Let's carry her and bring her in here," said Dakota.

"Still you haven't answered my question," said Keyon.

"Yes, two, I guess. She gave her mine too."

"You say she expected that you will sniff her plan but never to suspect she will load her with two," emphasized Keyon.

"Exactly. The first one was for real. This wiped us

out. Damn devil!" shouted Dakota.

Later that day a female scream echoed in the bunker. The other people stayed in their rooms away from Dakota. Keyon and Dakota were now seated in the other room examining the small device.

"Makes no sense. What do they want?" asked Keyon.

"Good question. Let's check what's missing," replied Dakota.

In the area near the coastline, a helicopter dropped two armed men. They advanced toward the city pointing guns as they proceed wearing face masks. They searched everywhere but the coastal city was deserted. There were signs of destruction everywhere with remnants of cars and buildings everywhere. There were limbs of people here and there. It was very horrific. Kyla in his thirties with short hair and Dante in his mid-thirties were scanning the city.

"Total wipeout! I repeat! No sign of life. Proceeding inside. Over!" said Kyla talking on the radio.

The two men headed further inside scanning every building and corner. The following day a helicopter hovered above but remained stationary in the air and the two men Keegan in his forties and Karson mid-thirties with a crew cut hair heavily armed slid down the ropes positioned as if ready to shoot anything. They picked up the bags as the helicopter hovered away. The beach area was deserted. The men heavily armed proceeded inside shooting everyone they come across who was still alive the massacre style. Their orders were to kill and clean the place. The sight was gruesome to watch as they were bodies scattered everywhere. Some of them getting second bullets once they have twitched or slightly moved. These people were part of those who had been in bunkers but somehow came out early. The men stared at each other before heading to the bank. The huge building in the city was the bank. Strangely to them, there was less resistance everyone was already down some seemed like they had choked to death. Anyone who showed any sign of life was shot dead. The cashier quickly spread her hands as if she had been blinded.

"Try nothing stupid! Move! Main computer frame?" asked Keegan.

Keegan held her shoulder pushing her, with the other hand holding the gun. A man was seated on the desk, but he seemed as if he could not see as well but instantly opened his eyes and looked at the men.

"Get down right now!" shouted Karson.

Keegan connected a device from his bag and pressed a button. A beep sound startled everyone. Audrianna in her thirties a brunette with short hair with a lovely curvy body was nursing Layleen before Dakota and Keyon entered the room.

"How is she doing?" asked Dakota.

"Raised temperature," she replied.

Dakota and Keyon quickly threw each other a quick glance. The two men left the room.

"I knew it. That must have happened when I removed the decoy," said Dakota.

"So, removing the booby-trap caused the leak?" asked Keyon.

"Exactly," he replied.

The people in the bunker gathered together. There were concerns and fears among the people and Dakota saw it fitting to address this once and for all. The two men addressed the people.

"Please don't panic. I want everyone to grab oxygen masks just as a precaution and can you go to the other rooms in the bunker. You have everything you need there and stay there for now. I want to reassure everyone that you have nothing to be afraid of. Kiara in his forties with long straight hair of medium built raised her hand.

"How long are we going to be here? Are we at risk why we need the oxygen masks?" she asked.

"One more day here the wind should clear the area, but we can stay here for as long as two weeks," replied Dakota.

A huge buzz filled the bunker.

"We have enough supplies," he added. Braydon a masculine man with a high fade taper haircut got up.

"Is there a risk of exposure? We can see that Layleen isn't feeling that good," he quipped.

Dakota cast an eye at Keyon and breathed heavily. He moved closer to Braydon.

"She lost a lot of blood, but we have safely removed the device. So, nothing to worry about, I assure everyone that everything will be okay," explained Dakota.

"Are there chances that this thing might explode in here and kill us all?" he asked further.

There was a moment of silence.

"If that was the case it could have detonated by now," Keyon further comforted everyone. Dakota and Keyon remain standing after everyone has dispersed.

"What's happening?" asked Keyon.

"I don't know they must have loaded that thing with electronic-viruses let's check," replied Dakota.

In the bunker, there was a research laboratory. The two men entered inside after wearing face masks. They were now in the small room of the bunker that was tightly sealed. They wore bodysuits.

"Damn it. We need an antidote fast. That must have happened when I removed the decoy, I mean the first booby trap. I must have damaged the seal.

"That could explain the fever. How much time do we have?" asked Keyon.

"Did you find out what's missing?" asked Dakota.

"They have looted all the money from all the five-coastal banks," replied Keyon.

Dakota stopped what he was doing and looked at Keyon.

"Money? So, it's a total wipeout. Which batches are remaining?" asked Dakota.

"Some twenty-seven-year-olds remain unexploded. Those above also who didn't get immunized by the previous government are still untouched," he replied.

The two men heard a knock at the door.

"It's Braydon," replied Dakota.

Keyon looked at Dakota with talking eyes.

"No, he is just concerned we all should be. So, are you saying they robbed all the five-coastal banks? Then released the viruses? What do they want?" asked Dakota confused.

Keyon paced in the lab for a while. He stopped and looked at Dakota.

"Protect the coastal borders. Send reinforcements. Secure oil resources. Clean the place then move in. Damn it. They are following your plan," shouted Keyon.

The men looked at each other for a while.

"Kaylynn. I taught her well. Now she is using my

plan against me," said Dakota.

The two men stared at each other.

"So, this is lethal. Total take over. We have only one antidote. Everyone will require at least one. I guess this is for Layleen," said Keyon.

"We are running out of time. They will send people to clean up soon. They are after the oil," said Dakota.

"I will go," said Keyon.

"You will die without the antidote," replied Dakota.

CHAPTER NINE

In the other territory, there is a lot of anticipation and hope and much expectation. The plan, as heard on the radio was a total success. The whole territory had been annihilated. The second team was sent to clean up the place. Some people had already begun celebrating. Kaylynn looked outside the window. "I just can't believe some people are still alive?" said Kaylynn.

"I am not surprised. Over the years they have created bunkers I guess," replied

Hayden.

"That means that Dakota could still be alive," added Kaylynn.

She frowned at the thought. Dakota was the last person she wanted to hear he was alive. This man would hinder her plans. He had been an obstacle in the past.

"I doubt it. Layleen could have finished the job and

there is no way he could have anticipated that," replied Hayden.

"I don't think it's a good idea to go there soon," added Hayden.

"Send the men to safeguard the oil. Get extra men around here too," ordered Kaylynn.

"You think he will come here?" asked Hayden surprised by the thought.

Kaylynn looked worried and not amused by all this. She knew there was a lot at stake.

"He is in love and will do anything for Layleen," replied Kaylynn.

Hayden looked confused for a split-second.

"Oh, I see. After the antidote?" he questioned.

"Exactly," replied Kaylynn.

"He will realize that I used his plan and put everything together," she added.

In the other territory, a few had been out of the bunkers. Dakota and Keyon had advised the people to remain inside the bunkers until further notice. Inside the bunker, Dakota and Keyon left the lab room. Braydon was still seated outside the lab by the time they got out. He stood up at their sight.

"How can I help? I can't just sit here. Surely there is a way I can help," he added.

The two men looked at each other and Dakota breathed with relief. He had assumed that Braydon wanted to complain and whine. He looked at Keyon.

"Someone must go to the oil plant," said Dakota.

"I can go. But I will need the jab," explained Braydon.

Dakota and Keyon looked at each other for a while.

"We have only one jab," replied Dakota.

"I will go. You stay here. Jab for Layleen. She needs it," replied Keyon.

Dakota and Braydon looked shocked. Dakota felt happy to hear that. There was no way he could have let the love of his life die especially when there was a way out. Braydon felt bad as they all realized that he only volunteered to go so he can get the jab. He looked down and apologized.

"Let's go together. You are right, the jab for the

lady," he offered his help.

The whole area was deserted no human life was evident. When night fell. Braydon left the bunker. Later at night he came out of the oil plant and called Dakota to let him know the mission was a success. They spoke for some time before Dakota went back to the bunker. Braydon walked to his car. He opened the door and instantly a car in front of him flashes its headlights. Instantly he was punched on the back of his head. He banged on the open door and a jab in the ribs left him in pain that he dropped on his knees. A further kick in the head left him partly dizzy. He saw a blurred figure that stamped on him. He lay down for a while before he grabbed the man's leg and twisted it. The man tumbled and fell next to him. He jumped onto him and ferociously delivered a series of left and right punches to the head. The clicking of a gun halted him instantly. He slowly got up and raised his hands up. The man on the ground got up and kicked him in the ribs. The man held Brayden's head by the hair and delivered a punch to the face. Instantly he blacked-out. Hours later heavy black smoke blew-up into the air rising high covering the once clear skies. Down on the ground level, the oil was burning ferociously. The whole night was lit with the flames of burning oil. The two men wearing face masks looked on as the oil ravaged in flames. Soon afterward they got in the car and drove off. Later the car swerved from left to right before spinning over a cliff and blowing into flames. Thick black clouds covered the dark skies giving the end of the world-feeling.

Far away Hayden was talking to Kaylynn.

"I received a message. The men we sent there have somehow choked to death," explained Hayden.

Kaylynn looked saddened and upset. She paced around swearing and cursing. She couldn't believe how Dakota was still alive.

"The place should be okay by now. How did this happen? Dakota must be alive. That son of a bitch," she cursed.

"Maybe he copied your style and retaliated?" suggested Hayden.

"Send our men to retrieve one and send him to the lab," ordered Kaylynn.

"I don't think it's a good idea. What if it is something more serious and we don't have an antidote for that?" asked Hayden.

"We need that oil the sooner the better," she replied.

A few days later there was a conference meeting at

the research lab. The Professor and the other scientists were in the conference room with Kaylynn and Hayden.

"Why people are dying at such a rate? Are you telling me that no one knows why? What am I paying you for? Hundred thousand people dead and no one knows why?" said Kaylynn.

There was silence for a while as everyone looked at each other.

"We think they have retaliated and created even stronger poisons than ours and all the people who have died have the old medical devices," replied the Professor.

Kaylynn looked at everyone and then at Hayden.

"Are you saying whatever it is its airborne?" asked Hayden.

"Precisely. The new medical device can purify the air itself that could explain why no one with the new device hasn't died yet," replied the Professor. Cynthia a thirty-four-year-old blonde girl entered the room breathing heavily.

"What is it Cynthia?" asked the Professor.

Everyone looked at her as she breathed heavily.

She rested to gather her breath and walked closer to the Professor.

"Professor! I know why!" she shouted with much delight. Everyone looked at her waiting for her to explain why.

Hayden too curious and impatient to wait talked to her.

"Go ahead we are listening," he remarked.

"They have laced the oil with a genetically changed virus. It's like a watermark or as a seal. I think you are using stolen oil. That is what is killing all these people," she added.

There was a moment of silence. No one said anything, but they all looked at Kaylynn. She looked at everyone and paced in the lab for a while.

"How come they are not dying on their side. Antidote?" she quizzed.

"Yes, they must have immunized everyone there years ago I guess," replied Hayden.

"You should stop using this oil until we have developed an antidote," suggested Cynthia.

"Damn it! Dakota. He laced the oil with viruses.

Bastard. What are we going to do? We need the oil otherwise everything will come to a standstill," shouted Kaylynn.

"If we keep on burning the fuel more people will die, I think Cynthia is right,"

explained the Professor.

Kaylynn sighed heavily and looked at Cynthia for a while.

"Can you work on the antidote?" asked Kaylynn.

"It takes time. Why not negotiate and buy the oil from them?" suggested Cynthia.

"You mean give them back their money?" hinted Hayden.

Kaylynn did not like the tone of how that sounded. She looked at Cynthia and at Hayden with talking eyes. If eyes could kill, they all could be dead by now.

"Or create a super virus then blackmail them into giving us the oil. Or exchange the antidotes," suggested the Professor.

That put a radiant look on Kaylynn's face. She smiled and looked at the Professor. Another look at

Hayden left a creased face on her.

"Good idea professor," she complimented him.

Hayden stood up really upset shaking with anger.

"You people. Everything about you is about viruses. You spend $ billion making viruses, are you fucking stupid? When will this end? You are like primitive people. All that money you should have invested it into research. Find other sources of energy maybe go to another planet. You fight each other creating viruses instead of finding a way of eradicating viruses. Look around you. You steal the world's money so you can make super viruses? These people are funding you to commit a crime against humanity does that make sense?" Hayden addressed the people. But such a move did not impress Kaylynn at all especially the way he talked to her in front of everyone. Kaylynn felt like an imprint was left on her heart by Hayden's action. Everyone could see the devil's rage in that beautiful face of hers. It was a few seconds before she exploded. The professor tried to slow that process, but it was too late. Kaylynn was shaking with rage. She got up and walked in front of everyone. She looked at Hayden with a blood-covered-face. "Don't talk to me like that ever again," she quipped.

Hayden realized his mistake and tried to make up

for it.

"Sh sh. Don't interrupt me when I am talking. OK?"

Hayden nodded his head.

"You forgot already! That they early wiped us off the face of the earth?" she asked Hayden.

She stopped and looked at everyone.

"What else do you expect when you rob their resources and their oil? All that money you spent making viruses you should have invested it into other energy resources. Look at you, you use viruses to control and manipulate others. It's only a matter of time before they retaliate. My main concern is that they will retaliate and create super viruses and wipes us out. I know you say you use these viruses to command and be obeyed but they are lethal to others. Everyone will see us as hostile and retaliate. Are we prepared? We are like petty thieves; these are just our survival skills. My question is this; does the others feel the same? Look nearly a hundred thousand dead already," pleaded Hayden.

The Professor tried to quench the fires, but it was too late. This time Kaylynn got really upset. Her once beautiful eyes filled with rage. She looked at Hayden with red eyes. Shaking like seaweed in the river being tossed around by a harsh breeze.

"An eye for an eye!" she shouted. She walked toward Hayden and looked at him in the eyes with scorn.

"Don't push me! You should be on my side no matter what," she fumed.

"You started it by robbing their oil and you then killed at will. You alone nearly

caused the extinction of humanity when will you stop?"

"Don't test me, Hayden, my patience is running out with you. Whose side are you on?" she fumed even more.

Hayden looked around and saw that everyone had left the room leaving them alone.

"There has been too much blood spilled for nothing. Blood of innocent women and children. I am tired of these wars. How many men let alone women and children died needlessly in the right's wars, in the oil wars and now you want to start a virus war!" shouted Hayden.

"What do you suggest?" asked Kaylynn.

"We negotiate if they refuse, we fight. For the love of God spare the women and children," pleaded Hayden.

Later that night Kaylynn seemed upset even when she tried to hide it. Every time she recalled Hayden's words she felt like suffocating with rage. Hayden was growing out of favor with her. He was too concerned with things she considered as petty. Kaylynn forced herself to sleep but just couldn't. At night she woke up and walked to the dressing table. She stopped and stared at Hayden who was sleeping peacefully. She stealthily opened the drawer. A tear ran down her cheek and she inched forward to where Hayden slept peacefully. He somehow instantly opened his eyes and saw Kaylynn standing next to him, staring at him.

"Are you okay darling?" he asked her.

Kaylynn remained silent. A tear dropped near Hayden. He instantly noticed a gun in Kaylynn's hand. He woke up and sat down on the bed.

"What is the matter with you," he asked not afraid at all.

"We don't share the same vision anymore. You humiliate me in front of everyone. No matter what, I told you, you must stick with me," she complained.

He breathed heavily.

"What is this about?"

"I want you to go there and kill Dakota but first give him so much pain until he tells you the oil antidote. Give him one chance if he refuses…," she paused and looked at him.

"You know the drill. Let him look for the antidote," she handed him a small tube.

Dakota was addressing the crowd.

"I think it's time we pay our friend a visit. They looted our money and our oil, but I think now they must have learned a lesson that looting is not good for them. I think they are weakened now. This is the best time for us to attack," said Dakota.

"You are all safe if you all stay in the bunkers. We shall sacrifice our resources. Our oil until we have won the battle. We shall keep the oil fires burning until they have surrendered. This shall be a deterrent so if you all stay here you will all be protected!" shouted Keyon.

"We want you all to stay indoors. We shall burn the oil for days and choke out enemies to death" added Dakota.

CHAPTER TEN

After the oil war, the Carolinadeivid territory although weakened by having their five- coastal banks robbed there was no invasion thanks to the burning of oil-laced with viruses. The only problem was that they had to keep burning the oil to deter invasion. Oil was going fast. They had to come up with a new plan. Maybe hire the deadliest assassin money can buy to deal with the corrupt and evil world. "We don't know how long we can sustain deterring them at a cost of losing oil resources or maybe we need to send an assassin," suggested Dakota.

Joycelyn in her forties a blond good-looking woman was now Dakota's second wife. She entered the building.

"I understand that the seven countries making the other territory have been tasked each with special functions. Even though they seem separate and as individual states, they work as one," advised Joycelyn.

"The first country it's task is to develop aerial and ground warfare. Then number two specializes in biochemical warfare. Number three in Cyberwarfare, etc. They are all in this together. This is why it's so widespread and difficult to control."

"You should negotiate, come together and build a stronger future," she added.

"They have evil engrave to the bone. Why would you steal everyone's resources just to make viruses to use on them later? That is just not acceptable." said Dakota.

"The world is fucked up. We spent $billions making viruses when people are dying because of a lack of basic needs," hinted Keyon.

"If you consider me as a friend would you spend $billions making viruses to use on me or you would build me a yacht, a car or something nice?" asked Dakota.

"Don't ask me. It's one man for himself and God for us all," said Keyon before he burst into laughter.

"God? But the God you are talking about also discouraged such evil practices. So, what do you say about that?"

"God gave every man a brain to use whatever resources are at your disposal to

enhance your life. Isn't that correct?" asked Keyon.

"That's correct but I am saying that women and children are dying needlessly. They are dying because of man-made viruses. That can never be tolerated no matter what. Population control or what no man has the right to wipe another man's using man-made viruses. The world should come together and fight this. If they were to be struck by lightning, I would not complain. It's wrong for people to spend billions of dollars making man-made viruses they use to control and kill women and children at will through immunization vaccines and the so-called medical devices. This should have been resolved a long time ago. Remember some seventeen years ago there was the rights-wars to address this. So why is this still happening now?" asked Dakota.

"I am just trying to make the argument seem balanced but there is no justification at all for making and using a lethal weapon that can kill women and children. Do you think if for the past 2000 years we were using viruses we still will be here today? The world should stand together. A person who thinks like this is every creature's enemy.

To war," toasted Keyon.

"I think there is a better way. We lost a lot of children and women. All my men are dead or incapacitated. I think we need a new way. We can't let the rotten eggs spoil the lot," Dakota paused and looked at Keyon.

Keyon squinted his eyes and looked at Dakota.

"What do you have in mind," asked Keyon.

"Target only the evil leaders they are the biggest terrorists. We must defend our rights and our way of life. I don't care if they are in power or not. Enough is enough. Send terror to fight terror! Get in the assassin!" shouted Dakota

A car screeched its tires skidding before making a U-turn in the road. Keyon revved the car and pulled a gun. He fired consecutive shots shattering the window screen. A man suddenly ducked. The car soon disappeared leaving the man shaken. Keyon entered the office carrying a bag. He opened the bag and took out his laptop and placed this on the table. He placed the assembled pole there. He walked back again and left another assembled pole. He took his gun and switched the poles indicators on. He looked at his watch. He synchronized the poles and waited. A beep sound was instantly released from the laptop. Keyon fired three consecutive shots and instantly the blue lights on the pole disappeared. The man left the building. Ayden walked into the building where he has an office and walked in the corridor going to his office. He was old in his early fifties, smartly dressed and wearing a suit. He was the head of the biochemical warfare. He entered his office and sat in his chair.

The phone rang with an anonymous caller identity. He answered the call.

"Is it morally correct to steal others' resources so that you make viruses to use on them later on?" asked the anonymous caller.

"We will do whatever it takes to defend ourselves," replied Ayden.

"What are the chances that women and children will end up being affected by your weapons say if you use them?" asked the anonymous caller.

"Slim," he replied.

"So, you're telling me that your weapons will only kill men?" quizzed the anonymous caller.

"Intended to be used on our enemies. Yes," replied Ayden.

"Would you say it's justified to make biological weapons having in mind that they nearly wiped us out and still killing others?"

"I am just doing my job," replied Ayden.

"Even if it means killing women and children unnecessarily?" asked the anonymous caller.

Silence for a while.

"Do you know the ten rules?" asked the caller.

"Listen find someone else to nag okay," said Ayden before putting the phone down.

Three bullet sounds rocketed the building. Ayden slumped onto the desk. Blood oozed from his head onto the desk and dripped down onto the floor. Kaylynn was watching the news with Broderick. A man in his mid-forties, handsome and of average build.

"We all know now that after the oil wars the other side laced the oil with synthetic viruses as a deterrent to looting. This has seen the introduction of small medical devices implanted on everyone to help with the purification of the air and fighting these viruses. Every time we use this fuel these viruses are released into the air. It seemed evil people have made viruses then feed them into these medical devices too and causing death and extorting thousands of dollars from the richest," said the anchorwoman.

Kaylynn flicked the channels.

"Just in! The head of the biowarfare company was shot dead. No one knows by who, but the footage has been released and according to local people a ghost has shot the man dead," Ester reporting.

"Is it true that a synthetic or electronic virus can be used with this device to cause death?" asked Broderick.

"Nothing is impossible," she replied.

Dakota is with Keyon.

"We must find a way, or we are toast," said Dakota.

"What do you mean?" asked Keyon.

"They have found a way of creating software that acts the same way as all the viruses.

Software that imitates all diseases" replied Dakota.

"Still nothing to worry about," said Keyon.

"Imagine an Mp3 player that vibrates. Then

massages and soothes your nerves," replied Dakota.

"Yeah," replied Keyon.

"Imagine also an MP3 player loaded with a viral software that causes havoc to your nerves. The device is used to load viruses as it vibrates to stress out nerves and cause diseases in the body," replied Dakota.

"So, this oil pollution thing is just a smokescreen?" asked Keyon.

"Yes, this was her idea anyway she had planned all this a long time ago," replied Dakota.

"You? What was your plan?" asked Keyon.

"Hayden. But she knew somehow and got rid of him. Maybe I should pay her a visit," suggested Dakota

Dakota traveled all night all the way to the other territory. Stealthily Dakota

contortion himself through the door. Quietly he tiptoed to where Kaylynn was sleeping.

"Where is Broderick? I was expecting you," said Kaylynn.

"Broderick is smoking outside," replied Dakota.

"And he let you come in here," asked Kaylynn doubting Dakota's account.

"I told him I am visiting a friend, he understood that a friend got to see a friend, right?" replied Dakota.

Kaylynn got up and lunged at Dakota who grabbed her.

"You killed my love. You must die too," said Dakota.

Kaylynn laughed first sarcastically.

"I gave you that lady, and you killed her yourself by disobeying me and turning her against me," replied Kaylynn.

"I did not lace-her with viruses, you did," explained Dakota upset.

"People die. Look you have a new wife already," replied Kaylynn.

"She gave me a present for you," said Dakota calmly.

Dakota put his arm across her shoulders and kissed her.

"I find it hard to tell you how she suffered I thought it's better for you to tell yourself who best to tell you than yourself," said Dakota kissing her in the head. Dakota walked out. Rage and pain exploded inside Kaylynn. She took out the gun and shouted at Dakota. Dakota stopped and turned around.

"Where do you think you are going? It's either you give me the antidote, or we go together!" she shouted shaking with anger.

Kaylynn aimed the gun at Dakota shaking with rage. Dakota smiled calmly that it got Kaylynn scared for a while.

"You think this is a joke?" asked Kaylynn.

"No. But it's not loaded. You gave me Layleen, and I gave you Hayden, but you killed him, so I gave you Broderick. He removed the bullets," replied Dakota.

Dakota turned around and walked away.

"Dakota! You son of a bitch stop before I shoot you in cold blood!" shouted Kaylynn trembling with anger.

Dakota laughed and stopped. He turned around and instantly a bullet jerked him very hard blowing him backward.

"You think I am joking? The antidote or you die first!" shouted Kaylynn raising the gun again for the second time.

"Ah Broderick," whispered Dakota to himself in a soft voice.

"I knew you would try to mess with me!" when are you going to learn.

She inched forward pointing the gun and shaking uncontrollably.

"I think it's better we die together. We have caused a lot of unnecessary suffering. If I let you live, I think God will punish me," said Dakota.

Kaylynn stopped and pondered all this.

"You fucking-bastard you would die and leave all this. Are you fucking mad? Your choice. Broderick or Keyon will tell me. Or I will kill all including Jocelyn your new wife," said Kaylynn.

Dakota got up holding his shoulder.

"The antidote is the blood of septuplets mixed

together followed by immersing yourself in a pool of oil," replied Dakota.

Kaylynn pointed a gun at Dakota and pushed him back into the house.

"Where are these septuplets?" asked Kaylynn.

Dakota laughed sarcastically.

"You believe this? Are you stupid? You will die just like everyone you killed. You think I will let you destroy septuplets just to save yourself. I am afraid not," replied Dakota.

"Don't play games with me or I will bloody shoot you!" shouted Kaylynn.

Dakota cast a mocking smile.

"You are not taking me seriously than you should do," said Kaylynn.

She instantly fired consecutive shots before Dakota slumped to the floor. She felt unwell, sweating and breathing heavily. She opened the clothes wardrobe and Broderick's body slumped onto the floor lifeless.

Kaylynn staggered to the research lab holding a gun. She leaned against the door and entered the lab. Later she was with the Professor. She was lying on the bed with drip tubes. The professor was running around making syrups to quench the poisons.

"Did he tell you the antidote?" asked the Professor.

Kaylynn smiled and looked at the Professor.

"That coward died I think he never got off what happened to Layleen. I guess I

reminded him of that lady he wanted to die with her," explained Kaylynn.

The Professor stopped and looked at Kaylynn.

"That fool thought he can kill you. Where is he now?" asked the Professor not

expecting any answers.

"He might have got what he wanted. If we can't find the antidote, then what?" Asked Kaylynn.

"What did he actually say maybe there is a hint for the antidote?" asked the Professor.

"He said he wanted me to feel what Layleen went through. I think same as Layleen's," replied Kaylynn.

"If same as Layleen then that's ours then we have the antidote. Okay, we try that and see but I asked because I don't want to sit and wait, I would rather be working on something else," replied the Professor taking his gear out.

Kaylynn scared for the first time in her life. She looked like she has seen a ghost.

"Something you want to tell me?" asked the Professor.

"He said I need blood of septuplets to remove the curse," explained Kayleen.

"What?" asked the Professor.

Miles away Keyon is with Dante a twenty-two-year-old geek and programmer.

"I have a big challenge for you. I have serial numbers I want you to locate these people see how fast you can triangulate them," said Keyon.

"You are not trying to make me hack into the FBI, are you?" asked Dante casting a serious face.

Keyon laughed mockingly.

"Don't make me laugh. As if you can," he replied.

"Do you want to bet?" asked Dante confident.

Keyon laughed the idea off.

"No that's okay just these for today. Okay?" he
requested.

The boy tried and tried but still failed. I can't break-
in. I need a government identity. Keyon drove away
from Dante's house and soon after he noticed that
an SUV was following him. The chase has begun. He
changed gears quick. He looked in the rear-view
mirror and saw the car closing in. The driver of the
car behind drove faster and bumped the back
bonnet of his car. He jerked forward losing control
of the car for a while. Instantly a bullet rocketed
smashing the back-window screen, but he had
already ducked. The horn blast by the oncoming
car gave his heartbeat a push. He pulled his gun
and fired backward swerving in the act. He turned
into a side road and stepped on the gas. Keyon
checked in the rear-view mirror. To his surprise,
the car was closing in faster. He stepped on gas
passing other cars. A bullet smashed the side
mirror. He ducked and lost control of the car. He
slammed on the brakes before bumping into a
parked car. The alarm of the parked car went off.
He quickly changed gears. A reverse gear clicked in
that he then looked over his shoulder and saw the
car approaching at full speed. He revved the car the

wheels spun in one place for a while blue smoke was coming from the tires. He reversed into the front bonnet of the car. He fired consecutive shots before spinning out of the car and blasting at the side door. He ducked, and fling opened the door. Surprise, surprise, the car was empty. He raised his head and scanned the area. He caught a quick glimpse of a man staggering away limping. He got up and aimed at the man. He then fired a shot at a low angle. He swiftly placed the gun down and breathed heavily.

A car suddenly parked outside Dante's house. Keyon opened the car door and walked out and into the yard of the house. I have this identity card; can you use this social security number? Dante grabbed the card and entered codes after codes. Keyon dozed off before a beep went off.

"We are in! I don't know for how long though. What are you after?" asked Dante excited.

"Link these serial numbers to name, face, place, current location, medical file, spouse, kids, dogs, cats I mean everything. Load on here when done," Keyon smiled and looked at Dante.

After a few minutes, a message appeared on the screen.

Message on the screen.

Three minutes before automatic shutdown.

"How many you got so far?" asked Keyon checking the status after some time.

"Just 4," he replied.

"4 only! Come on! I need all, okay?" hinted Keyon.

Dante typed quick. A message instantly appeared on the screen. The only 60 seconds left a message on the screen startled him. He stopped and looked at Keyon. The countdown has begun.

Message on screen.

45 seconds,

30 seconds,

15 seconds,

Dante sweat. When there were only three seconds left, the screen froze.

"How many?" asked Keyon.

"6!" replied Dante.

The system suddenly shut down.

"OK we will find out who is the lucky one," Keyon looked at Dante.

Keyon took a tablet from his jacket. He retrieved a screen pen and inserted the memory card.

Instantly the list appeared on the screen. Matching their faces to their current location.

"Do you want to play?" inquired Keyon.

"Is that a game?" asked Dante.

Keyon smiled and replied.

"Yes, press the button every time the picture comes into the target area," advised Keyon.

It took a while before a target was gained. Dante pressed the button, and a splash appeared on the screen.

"Only five remain!" shouted Dante hysterically.

"Play until you have blown all up. Thanks," said Keyon. He got up to leave. Dante concentrated.

Jocelyn was at home watching the news.

"It is understood that five leaders of the company

that makes synthetic and software viruses which they use to abuse women and children were blown up in their homes in front of their families and kids. It comes after the court ruling that they had to stop and close with immediate effect. The submitted claims and the court costs will bankrupt them. This should be a lesson to those who think they are above the law. In this edge, there is nothing more important than good health and life of women and children. Those who think they can make a quick dosh at the expense of kids and women watch out the Trigger-man is coming to blow you up," said the anchorwoman.

Keyon watched the news as he was making dinner. He stopped and listened to the news.

"Pick up! Pick up!" shouted Keyon.

The phone rang, but no one picked up the phone. Keyon grabbed his jacket and opened the drawer and got a spare gun. He quickly drove off. Tapping his fingers nervously on the steering wheel. His heart beating fast. He passed other cars most of the time ignoring the traffic lights. He dialed again. He slammed on the brakes and parked the car. He stealthily entered the yard looking everywhere pointing a gun.

Nervously he inched forward, his heart beating quick with every step.

He slowly slid the door open. Stealthily he tiptoed inside the house. He could see Dante watching the television in the lounge. Instantly he felt the barrel of a gun poking his head. It's the Bad guy in his forties smartly dressed up though.

"Drop the gun! Move! Don't try anything stupid," ordered the Bad guy.

The bad guy hit him and pushed him onto the couch pointing a gun at him.

"Enter your password," Keyon entered the password and when he was about to give the tablet back, he dropped it. The man kneeled his gun pointing at Keyon. He looked down briefly for a moment that's when Keyon grabbed and twisted his hand. He then kicked the man in the face.

"Dante! Pick up the tablet finish the game! You! {referring to the Bad guy} Hands up!"

Dante said nothing but looked at Keyon.

"Dante, finish the game!" shouted Keyon.

Instead, he folds his lips and pointed at the man.

"Oh, I see. You don't want him to spoil your carpet ha?"

Dante nodded his head.

"Move! Go outside now! Move!" shouted Keyon. The man walked outside before being pushed by Keyon.

"Who is the seventh person in your organization?" asked Keyon pointing a gun at the Bad guy.

"If I tell you will you let me go?" asked the Bad guy.

"Are you fucking mad? You nearly crippled this lad and if I hadn't turned up, he would have witnessed another accident isn't it?"

"So, you don't want to know?"

"Okay you tell me, and we will let the lad decide okay?" He looked at the man.

"We are a cult if you want to call it. Each one has separate responsibilities. I manage finance and money collection.

"Hilarious. Is that how you call daylight robbery," asked Keyon.

"We provide a service and like everyone else, we expect to be paid but if they don't pay, then no one cares they end up tripping or falling or just having a bad day," says the bad guy.

"No, you force your services on people who do not need them," replied Keyon.

"The name?" asked Keyon.

Keyon jerked backward hit in the face by fluids of the bad guy. He wiped blood off his face and stared at Dante, then cast a cheeky smile.

"Guess you couldn't wait ha? Can't blame you. Introducing the young Trigger-man. All you evil leaders out there be careful the young Trigger-man is impatient."

Keyon smiled looking at Dante.

"So, am I an Assassin now?" asked Dante smiling.

"The deadliest Assassin money can buy," replied Keyon.

"Okay give me more serial numbers we blow up some more. Come!" shouted Dante dragging Keyon in the house.

Keyon stopped and looked at Dante.

"What is wrong? Come let us blow more bad guys."

"Dakota said only the evil cult leaders for now. The real big terrorists. Manipulating, terrorizing and controlling the innocents. See if the eggs will remain fresh."

Dante twisted his mouth.

"But I am still the deadliest Assassin money can buy. Right?" asked Dante.

"Definitely. The deadliest Assassin money can buy. I just need more serial numbers then we are on. Okay?"

Dante smiled and ran into the house.

"The deadliest Assassin money can buy. Waal!" shouted Dante.

---To Be Continued—

THE END

ABOUT CAROLINADEIVID

176

I am a new author with an interesting writing style that keeps you on the edge of the seat leaving you wanting more. Check out my other books:

The Vice President The Trillionaire

The Vice President Directive 17: The Origins.

The Vice President The War Directive: When War Is The Only Option.

The Vice President The Electronic Transfer: Volume 1

The Vice President The Electronic Transfer: Volume II The Death Trap.